Dear
Manny

Also by Nic Stone

Dear Manny

NIC STONE

Crown
New York

Text copyright © 2025 by Logolepsy Media Inc.
Jacket photograph of boy copyright © 2025 by Nigel Livingstone
Interior retro sky pattern art by Vlntn/stock.adobe.com
Interior paper texture art by paisan191/stock.adobe.com
Interior adhesive tape art by YummyBuum/stock.adobe.com

All rights reserved. Published in the United States by Crown Books for Young Readers, an imprint of Random House Children's Books, a division of Penguin Random House LLC, 1745 Broadway, New York, NY 10019.

Crown and the colophon are registered trademarks of Penguin Random House LLC.

Visit us on the Web! GetUnderlined.com

Educators and librarians, for a variety of teaching tools, visit us at RHTeachersLibrarians.com

Library of Congress Cataloging-in-Publication Data is available upon request.
ISBN 978-0-593-30801-1 (trade)—ISBN 978-0-593-30802-8 (lib. bdg.)—
ISBN 978-0-593-30803-5 (ebook)

The text of this book is set in 11.3-point Adobe Garamond Pro.

Printed in the United States of America
10 9 8 7 6 5 4 3 2 1
First Edition

For those who keep growing

Hello again, beloved reader!

I know, I know: *Another* book in what I guess is now officially a trilogy? And with a *white* boy on the cover?! What gives?!

Well, in the seven-ish years since *Dear Martin* was published, I've encountered a gloriously wide range of young people who read and were moved by it. Through emails and messages and letters from and conversations with them, I've come to realize three universal truths:

1. Being a person is hard.

2. Being a person in relationship with other people is harder.

3. Being a person in a multicultural world where you have to be in relationship with *lots* of people, many of whom look, think, feel, and believe differently than you do, is the hardest thing of all.

Number three feels especially true right now. (Just turn on the news if you don't believe me.) And yet here we all are: trying to figure out not only how to survive, but how to thrive *and* to do the most good in a world full of other people.

The same is true for young men like Justyce McAllister, Quan Banks, and Jared Peter Christensen (that's who's on the cover of this book): Despite being from very different walks of life, all three of these young men have done the best they can with the information they have about the cards they've been dealt. What makes the difference is what they decide to do with those cards once they get *new* information.

When we met Jared Peter Christensen in *Dear Martin,* he was entitled and annoying. In *Dear Justyce,* he . . . was still entitled and annoying. BUT he'd pulled himself together a smidge and was trying to be helpful.

Now, in his very own book, we get to see how much he's grown . . . or not. Either way, he wouldn't shut up until I wrote it.

Hope you dig.

Two years, two months, and three days prior

Jared let the first two calls go to voicemail, and he outright silenced the third. But then there was a fourth. Which meant there would be a fifth. Blake Benson, one of Jared's closest friends since elementary school (though lately Jared had begun to wonder why) was nothing if not persistent.

But Jared didn't want to talk. He was still too angry from the fight with his supposed *best* friend.

He picked up anyway. If for no other reason than to tell Blake to stop calling.

"DUDE, WHY AREN'T YOU ANSWERING MY CALLS?!" were the first words out of Blake's mouth. Because of course: No matter what Blake had been calling about the first (and second . . . and third . . .) time, the fact that Jared hadn't picked up was now the most important thing. The word *entitled* rang through Jared's head. It had been spat at him with the force of a bullet by the one person Jared *used to* feel safe always being himself around.

And if that hadn't hurt enough, the fist to the jaw that followed certainly had.

"Bro," Jared said into the receiver. The word felt strange to his ears, but he shook it off. "I dunno what you want, but I'm really not in the mood—"

A *booop!* in Jared's ear signaled another incoming call. He looked to see who it was and was so surprised by the name and photo on the screen, he couldn't do anything but stare. Sarah-Jane Friedman had to be the person who hated Jared the most. Why would she be calling him?

"Hello?! EARTH TO CHRISTENSEN!" Jared was glad he didn't have the phone to his ear now because Blake was yelling. Jared despised being yelled at. He got enough of it from his dad . . . Really didn't need it from a friend—

Sarah-Jane's face popped up again.

"Dude, I'll call you back," Jared said into the receiver before tapping to answer the other call without waiting for a response.

"Hello?"

"Jared?" SJ sounded far more panicked than Jared was expressly comfortable with.

"I mean, that is who you called." The moment the words were out of his mouth, Jared wished he could snatch them back. He got snarky when nervous, a defensive tic from years of being bullied by a monster of an older brother. He never *meant* to sound like a *condescending prick*—that was another thing that his (ex?) best friend had called him—but apparently his intentions didn't matter.

"I'd really like to hang up on you right now, but I'll take it from your typical asshole tone that you have no idea what's going on. Which sucks on *so* many levels."

That gave Jared pause. *What's going on . . .* The hell did that mean?

What came out of Jared's mouth: "Why does it suck?"

"I didn't wanna be the person to tell you."

"To tell me what?"

She didn't respond immediately. Which created just enough time for panic like nothing Jared had ever felt before to spread through his midsection and up into his throat like viscous black smoke.

"There was a shooting, Jared," SJ began.

And Jared knew what was coming. He could *feel* it. He'd seen the stories time and time again on social media . . . and looked away.

". . . at a traffic light," SJ was saying. "An off-duty cop . . ."

Something like static filled Jared's mind. And only three words cut through:

". . . didn't make it."

"I gotta go," Jared said. "My dad is calling me."

And he hung up.

There was a click and subsequent whirring sound in his mind. Like a highlight reel turning on. Short scenes from the past few weeks flashed through Jared's mind, each one more torturous than the one before: his stomach twisting when Blake tossed out the n-word at his birthday party (something Jared had never done—though he'd admittedly *thought* it a time or two), but coming to Blake's defense anyway. Because who did Justyce

McAllister think he was making a scene in a space that didn't belong to him?

Being panicked when Justyce started swinging, and relieved when he stormed out . . . but also nervous as hell and a little angry too when Manny—who was supposed to be *Jared's* best friend—decided to go after Justyce.

Feeling a pang of rejection at the county fair a few days later when Manny didn't laugh at Jared's joke. It'd been a little mean, yeah: There was a Black woman with five kids in tow who were all different complexions, so he'd made a comment about multiple baby daddies. All the other guys (who, yes, were white like Jared) thought it was hilarious, but Manny got offended and turned sullen. Jared obviously knew Manny was Black—he did have *eyes,* after all. But that hadn't ever seemed to matter before Manny started hanging out with Justyce (who, yes, was also Black).

And then there was the sensation of all the breath *whooshing* out of Jared's lungs when Manny body-slammed him on the gym floor four days ago. Breath he hadn't had time to regain before a jolt of pain shot through Jared's sinuses as Manny's fist connected with Jared's face. Again: Jared had made a joke. Yeah, it hearkened back to slavery or whatever (Jared may or may not have referred to himself as *massah* and suggested that Manny needed his permission for something). But slavery was long over, and Manny's parents were literally the most successful people Jared knew. The guy got a *brand-new* flossed-out Range Rover for his *fifteenth* birthday—so he could learn to drive using the vehicle he'd be driving once he got his license—which meant the joke was utterly preposterous. Manny's family could've bought *Jared.* That's what made the whole thing funny (to Jared, at least).

The words Manny shouted at Jared—*racist, bigot, privilege, entitled, condescending, prick*—hurt more coming from him than the punches did. Manny *knew* Jared. They'd literally grown up together. Jared's dad treated Manny more like a son than he treated Jared sometimes. And Manny's mom taught Jared to use a washcloth and put on lotion when he got out of the shower.

They were *family.*

Jared's phone rang again. Kyle this time.

He silenced the call, then shut the whole thing off.

An *"off-duty cop,"* SJ said. Hadn't Justyce had a run-in with a cop earlier in the school year? Something to do with Melo Taylor being drunk and Justyce looking like he was trying to carjack her? Jared found the whole thing ridiculous at the time: Justyce was the most straitlaced guy Jared knew. It was why he thought it'd be funny for Justyce to dress up like a gang member for their group Halloween costume: Nothing could've been further from the truth about the guy.

Another thing Jared thought was stupid at the time: SJ Friedman's insistence that Justyce's wrongful arrest had something to do with race.

But now . . .

"There was a shooting, Jared . . . at a traffic light. . . ."

Jared turned to look in the mirror attached to his dresser. His black eye from the fight with Manny had faded to a putrid yellow-green.

"Didn't make it . . ."

Jared's eyes narrowed, and his face throbbed. There was no way those words meant . . . They couldn't. It wasn't possible. Couldn't be. No, Justyce McAllister wasn't Jared's favorite person, and no,

Jared and Manny hadn't exactly been getting along lately, but still: They were *good* guys. Excellent ones, in fact.

In many ways, Jared knew, they were better than him.

Which meant that what SJ said could *not* be true. These sorts of things didn't happen to good guys. Not unless they'd done something wrong . . .

But what if they hadn't? The words rang through Jared's head like a scream.

Because he knew. The moment SJ said the word *shooting,* Jared knew Justyce and Manny—the only two Black guys in their graduating class—hadn't done anything wrong.

Which meant . . .

Jared took in his appearance: the brown hair, green eyes, vaguely tan skin that (still) qualified him as *white.*

But that didn't *really* matter . . .

Did it?

ACT I

Democracy Now!

1

We the People

Jared Peter Christensen is questioning his life choices.

Again.

(You'd think the guy would learn, considering how many idiotic binds he's gotten himself into over the years, but apparently not.)

Granted, the thing he's gotten himself into this time isn't *stupid*, necessarily. Just . . . not super well thought out. That's the reality smacking him upside the head as he sits in an exceedingly boring meeting he decided to attend a mere seven minutes before it started. Which then involved a sprint across campus that left him out of breath and *extra* conspicuous when he came in four minutes late.

He reads the slide currently on the screen behind the head of the sitting UCC president—a pretty Korean American girl named Ari Park, who is droning on at the podium:

Undergraduate College Council

MISSION STATEMENT:

To accurately represent the voices, perspectives, and concerns of all undergraduates while protecting their rights and freedoms.

His eyes drift to the door . . . but of course he can't walk out early after walking *in* late. He also put his name on that damn list, which, as Dad would say, means he has officially committed himself to this path. "Your name in your handwriting is a declaration that you'll see something through," Bill Christensen said to six-year-old Jared when he made him sign his first contract. It bound him to a set of chores in exchange for the funds that went into a 529 college savings plan.

Jared sighs and shakes his head. The regret is too real.

How did he even get here?

The slide changes to an overdone graphic listing college policy changes the Undergraduate College Council has enacted since its founding.

It's really his Constitutional Law professor Dr. Yeh's fault. Just before dismissing class earlier, she made it a point to announce that the UCC would be holding its first meeting for class officer elections. And she looked right at Jared as she said it.

He could swear she was *challenging* him. Especially since the look came on the heels of a class discussion about the current state of democracy. One that may have gotten a little heated at the end. Jared hadn't really meant to "go off," as one of his Black classmates put it, but he also couldn't sit there in silence as the guy who became his nemesis on the first day of class—an asshat-and-a-half "blue-blooded Florida boy" (his words) named John Preston LePlante IV—acted like *he* wrote the Constitution and could change it at will. The whole exchange is seared into Jared's memory:

John Preston: You guys are so stuck on some perceived threat to voting rights, you're missing the forest for the trees. The truest threat to our *republic* is getting so far away from the values this country was founded on, the nation itself becomes unrecognizable.

Imani: And what are those values, John Preston?

(Imani Williams is one of three Black students in the class. Living with an African American roommate who survived both a wrongful arrest *and* a police shooting their senior year of high school makes it impossible for Jared not to notice these things.)

John Preston: That question just proves my point. Only a person with *zero* concept of what it means to be American would ask that.

Imani: Me asking you to clarify your assertion with specific examples means I have "zero concept" of what it means to be American?

John Preston: I'm just saying if you knew, you wouldn't have to ask. As such, that question isn't worthy of an answer.

Jared: [*Officially furious.*] Dude, you deciding someone's very valid question "isn't worthy of an answer" is precisely the opposite of civility and open-mindedness. Both of which were "American values" at some point. I know we're talking about the Constitution, but if you read the Declaration of Independence, the bulk of the colonists' gripes with the king came from him having an attitude like yours.

Imani: [*Snapping her fingers.*] Go off then, Jared!

In the moment, her approval made Jared's heart grow three sizes, à la the Grinch. He had to resist thanking her out loud, and he knows he turned very red. But then Dr. Yeh made her little election-interest-meeting announcement. And she'd eyeballed the crap out of Jared when she said the words *Junior Class Council president.*

He tried to let it go. He really did. Shoved it out of his mind, went to his other two classes, and even popped by the frat house. But the moment he was alone in his apartment, all Jared could think about was Dr. Yeh's eagle-eyed stare.

A door opens behind him, and Jared fights the urge to look over his shoulder as Ari goes on to her next slide: another over-done graphic listing the SLOs (student-led organizations) the UCC works with.

Man, what is he *doing* here?

The screen goes dark (*thank god!*) and the lights in the room brighten as Ari asks if there are any questions. Jared's tempted to raise his hand just to make it seem like he was paying attention— Christensens *commit* once they're committed. But then a girl in the first row shoots her arm into the air with the velocity of a UFC punch, and someone slides into the folding seat to the left of Jared.

"Hi!" the girl says with far too much enthusiasm. "I'm a rising sophomore and I intend to seek election for SoCo president? Just wondering if you could give us a brief intro to the *history* of the UCC and its structure?"

"Well, the organization was founded in 1972," Ari begins with resignation in her voice, "but as we're short on time, we'll save our discussion of structure for the orientation meeting. Your attendance will be mandatory since you intend to run for an elected office."

"Also, that information is online," comes a low, disgruntled reply from Jared's left. "Meaning these 'mandatory' meetings are unnecessary and we could all be doing more productive things with our time."

At the sound of that voice—very bag of nails in a blender—Jared's stomach drops.

He turns.

Beside him is the last person on earth he'd want to see at a UCC information meeting: John Preston LePlante IV.

Jared sighs. Of *course* this guy showed up. Jared will never forget his first encounter with John Preston: Jared was walking past the tables for student-led organizations—excuse him: *SLOs*—set up on the quad during orientation week when someone called out and beckoned him over. Why he went, Jared still doesn't know, but he wound up in front of an overly preppy guy with an unironic crew cut. "You look like one of us, man," John Preston said, totally sizing Jared up. "Consider joining our ranks, yeah?" And he handed Jared a card with a QR code on it.

Jared had no idea what to think. Was this what it felt like to be profiled?

It rattled him, but of course Jared's curiosity got the best of him. The code led to an encrypted website, where he had to complete a five-question quiz that he later realized centered on the Confederacy. (And he felt deeply ashamed that he'd blazed right through it.) At the top of the next page was John Preston LePlante IV's picture as the "Founder and Chief Officer" of a collection of students who called themselves the Vineyard Traditionalists. Students on a mission "to return the Ivies to their former prestige through the reclamation and reestablishment of their founding standards and traditions."

It wasn't lost on Jared that every member pictured was similar to John Preston in both skin tone and gender identity. (Similar to Jared too, but he tried to ignore that part.)

John Preston grins at Jared, then faces forward. "I thought that was you, Christensen," he says. "You plan to run for something?"

Jared truly cannot stand this butt nugget. "Guess you'd know if you actually showed up on time and signed in."

"I see we're feeling spicy today!" John Preston says. "I've decided to run for Junior Class Council president."

Jared's throat tightens, but he refuses to let the discomfort show. Especially since he doesn't know why he's uncomfortable: John Preston LePlante IV is a clown and a half. "I genuinely couldn't care less, dude," Jared replies.

"I figured you'd say that." John Preston crosses his arms. "And this is precisely why I've decided to run. Our once-eminent institution is going to hell in a handbasket under the leadership of people like her." He jerks his prominent chin at Ari. "But what's *really* unfortunate is that guys like you don't give a damn."

Jared opens his mouth to respond, but in what is surely an act of divine intervention, the meeting is dismissed. So he stands and grabs his bag instead.

"Leaving so soon?" John Preston says.

"Meeting's over, bro."

"Aww, but our conversation was just starting!"

Jared doesn't reply. Just narrows his eyes as he forces himself to (calmly) climb to the exit at the top of the room.

Once he's out, he picks up the pace. Weaving around other students—*Are the hallways in this building always so crowded?!*—he moves as quickly as he can without looking like an idiot. Even bumps the shoulder of a Black girl headed in the opposite direction and keeps going. ("My bad," he says, doing his best to ignore the look of disgust on her face.) His chest has tightened, and he needs to get out of there.

Because Jared knows he can't back out now. Knows it like he knows that anything John Preston LePlante IV proposes will be aimed at keeping people like John Preston LePlante IV at the top of the food chain.

If *that* guy is the rising junior class's other presidential option, there's only one thing for Jared to do:

He's gotta win.

2

Self-Evident Truths

Jared pauses outside the door to his on-campus apartment and takes a deep breath. On his way home from the UCC meeting, he learned that Darius "D'Squared" Danielson, their university's star running back, has been expelled following a drunk-driving incident two nights ago that involved a campus cop crashing his bike into a tree and dislocating a shoulder.

The whole thing makes Jared very uncomfortable. He passed the scene on foot not even five minutes after leaving a party at the frat house . . . where *he* was drinking.

Something Jared would never tell anyone: His first (inebriated) thought when he saw Darius in handcuffs? *Thank god.* Because it meant the cops were too preoccupied to notice swaying, bleary-eyed Jared. There was no question *his* blood-alcohol content was above the 0.08 legal limit. No, he wasn't operating a motor vehicle, but he certainly wasn't supposed to be drinking: In addition to being underage, his driver's license was already suspended from his own alcohol-related driving snafu eleven months prior. So yeah: Getting caught wasted wouldn't have been a great look.

Thing is, as D'Squared told it, the good officer, who'd been traveling in the opposite direction, was drifting into his driving lane. When D'Squared—who was perfectly lucid (even the other cops admitted that)—honked to get the officer's attention, the officer overcorrected and ran himself off the road.

The worst part, though: A Breathalyzer test put D'Squared's blood-alcohol content at 0.04—*half* the legal limit to drive. But he was a week from turning twenty-one. Which, under Connecticut law, meant he got slapped with a DUI anyway.

So in addition to the expulsion, his NFL dreams are officially kaput.

Jared sighs. It bothers him to no end that the cops decided to Breathalyze a "perfectly lucid" Ivy League student, but he's trying not to think about that too much. Because he knows that when he walks into the apartment, if his roommate Justyce McAllister is home and has heard about D'Squared's expulsion, Justyce is gonna be plenty pissed and may not even *look* at Jared.

Because D'Squared, like Justyce, is a Black guy. One who has experienced firsthand how "consequences" can be impacted by a variable like "skin tone."

Jared, unfortunately, is evidence walking.

He braces himself and steps inside.

A *Briiiiiiing! Briiiiiiing! Briiiiiiing!* chimes from the living room TV. It makes Jared smile despite having no idea what mood

Justyce is in. There's no sound more sacred after a long day than that of Mario Kart coins being collected in earnest.

"Yo, you gotta get on this," Justyce says without looking up. So he *hasn't* heard about D'Squared. Jared exhales. (He's certainly not gonna be the person to tell him.) "Latest wave of booster courses dropped today, and it's this one through the heart of a volcano. . . ." His eyes go wide, and he shakes his head. "Woooooo boy! Hella banana peels, though. Which is a li'l random but— Oh snap!"

Jared's eyes lock onto the TV screen and he watches Justyce's driver—Mario, per usual—hit one of said peels and spin out, tumbling over the edge of the thin road straight into the roiling magma.

"Curves are a little tricky," Justyce says.

Jared doesn't respond. He's too transfixed by the red-orange liquid. All because of something *else* Justyce said to him once: *"I'm telling you, bro, being Black in this world feels like a never-ending game of The Floor Is Lava. One wrong move, and you're a goner."*

Is D'Squared not living proof of that?

The image on the screen freezes.

"Helloooo? Earth to Jared? You alive over there, dawg?"

Jared startles. "Huh?"

"You good? Your face is hella pale right now. You find another album of incriminating pictures at your fraternity house or something?"

"Huh?"

"You don't remember? There was apparently a *physical* photo album full of white people wearing wildly offensive Indigenous Peoples' costumes?"

"Oh god." Jared shudders. He does, in fact, remember. The frat had thrown a "Columbus DAY PARTY" a few years ago, and the photos were . . . Yeah. It was long before Jared rushed, but still. He'd seen enough stories about people's lives being shredded—jobs lost, college acceptances rescinded, associates publicly disassociating—over not-well-thought-out crap they'd said or done in the past. And though he isn't *in* any of the pictures, he knows being a member of the fraternity could cause him some problems were the pictures to ever get out. "Let's never bring that up again."

Justyce nods. "Got it. Well, come hop on the game and get some blood back in your mug, man. The ghost skin thing is giving me the creeps."

Jared drops his bag and takes his regular seat on the sofa, and Justyce hands him a controller and restarts the game. Jared, of course, chooses his regular driver: green-capped Luigi. "Something that's not lava, please," he says as Justyce begins scrolling through all the courses they can choose from.

He goes with a pirate's island.

As the race gets underway—Luigi falls behind quickly, which puts him on track to consistently trail his big bro—Jared realizes this course isn't super helpful either: all he can think about as chests full of treasure come flying in his direction is how people who look like Justyce were forced onto ships and brought to "the New World" to work without pay. By people who look like him. Did pirates ever attack slave ships?

He's gotta get it together.

"So?" Jus says, chopping into Jared's thoughts.

Jared's tempted to say "Huh?" again, but instead sits up

straighter and swerves Luigi around a flying skull. Tries to recenter himself. "I went to an info meeting for the Undergrad College Council."

"Oh ho! You poppin' into politics, my boy?"

"I'm thinking about it," Jared replies.

Which makes Justyce snort. "You put your name on a list for something?"

Princess Peach passes Luigi in her pink go-kart and hurls a banana peel over her shoulder. It smacks him right in the face just like Justyce's question does. Jus knows Jared far too well. "Yeah," Jared says. "I did."

"So, you're poppin' into politics then."

Jared sighs. "Guess I am."

"And you have regrets? Oh shit—" Justyce's body jerks right as he moves in tandem with his go-kart to dodge a shell hurled by Bowser. As the megalomaniacal mega-turtle turns and smiles triumphantly, it occurs to Jared how much the spike-shelled monster reminds him of John Preston LePlante IV.

Who he knows he *cannot* lose to . . .

But still. "Bro, I don't know what the hell I was thinking," Jared says honestly.

"*Were* you thinking, Jared?"

"Do you *have* to kick me when I'm down?" A giant grinning bullet smacks Luigi, and the go-kart spins into oblivion before blinking back to life on the track. In last place.

Justyce laughs. "Let's not get into victim mentality, man. You're in it now. So what's the move?"

It's an excellent question. And one Jared doesn't have an answer to. He realizes *just* how stupid this whole idea is. *Why did he put his name on that list?*

"It's for Junior Class Council president," he says. "Which, according to the website, involves representing the interests of the junior class." His eyes narrow. "But apparently also the wider student body? The sitting UCC president kept talking about *policy creation and enactment—*"

A mental lightbulb turns on. "You ever think about the Declaration of Independence?"

"*WOW.* Might be time for some ashwagandha and chamomile tea, buddy."

"I'm serious," Jared says. "We were talking about it in Constitutional Law—"

"Ain't that the class you call 'the bane of your collegiate existence'?"

"Yes, but that's irrelevant right now," Jared continues. "The Declaration of Independence came up today, and the part about governments 'deriving their just powers from the consent of the governed' really got under my skin."

"Why's that— Whoa!" Wario cuts right in front of Mario, and Justyce has to swerve.

"I'm not entirely sure yet," Jared admits, "but it made it click for me that elected leaders are supposed to *represent* the people they lead, not make decisions for them. There was a super asinine comment from that idiot classmate I complain about—"

"John Presley what's-his-face?"

Jared has told Justyce all about Jolly Pickle LePunkass. "Preston LePlante. But yeah, him. One of our Black classmates asked a perfectly valid question, and he acted like it delegitimized her U.S. citizenship."

"Well, damn."

"He's running against me, by the way."

Justyce pauses the game and looks at Jared. "Bury the lede much?"

"My bad," Jared says. "But yeah. I was the only name on that list before he got there, so he's my sole opponent."

"Welp." Justyce unpauses and the race resumes. "Definitely gotta stay in there now."

"Tell me about it. And the way he acted at the info meeting just—"

Justyce's phone pings on the arm of the sofa. He glances at it, frowns, then stops the game again to pick it up.

Jared's heart drops into his intestines and he stops breathing. Is Jus learning about D'Squared's expulsion right here in front of him?

"You gotta be friggin' *kidding* me," Jus says.

And *great*. Jared shuts his eyes and braces himself. "What happened?"

At first, Justyce doesn't respond. And as the silence stretches on, Jared could swear it condenses and begins to curdle like spoiled milk. He takes a deep breath and forces himself to meet Justyce's eyes.

Except he can't. Because Justyce is just staring straight ahead. "You good, man?" Jared asks.

"Nah," Jus replies. "I'm really not."

"You . . . gonna tell me why?"

After a few more loooooong seconds of torturous quiet, Justyce's shoulders droop and his chin hits his chest. Jared's anxiety shifts to concern. "Justyce?"

"Sorry, man. Hard to find words." Jus shakes his head and shuts his eyes. "I know this isn't something that really matters to *you,* so my reaction isn't gonna make sense—"

"Can you just tell me what happened, man?"

"Yeah." Justyce looks up and meets Jared's eyes. "The Supreme Court just struck down Affirmative Action."

March 28

Dear Manny,

First, let's address the elephant in the room: Is it weird as hell to be writing a letter to my dead best friend? Yes. Weirdest thing I've ever done. And as we both know, I've done some WEIRD shit. (Remember the Tide Pod dry ice bomb experiment? Iconic.)

But life is feeling a little out of hand these days, and Justyce—who made it clear that he "will continue to love me to death" but is "struggling to navigate Black life at this 'elite' institution of high ed" and therefore "lacking the bandwidth, time, and training to hold space for your feelings AND mine"—suggested I start "a journal of letters to someone who can't respond" and then told me about the one he wrote to Dr. King when we were seniors.

Did it feel great to have the person on this campus who knows me best emotionally abandon me in my time of need? Not at all. But I also know I can't really "get" what he's going through. So here we are. Nice to be . . . uhhh . . . communicating with you in the Great Beyond?

Before I jump in, let me update you on me. I've changed a lot since you died. (That felt strange to write, even though it's been almost three years.)

Actually, it's more accurate to say I changed BECAUSE you died. I won't get into it too much here, but what happened to you really woke me up, for lack of a better phrase. Ever since I got that phone call letting me know you "didn't make it," I haven't been able to stop noticing all the stuff the two of you and Sarah-Jane (she and Justyce are still going strong, by the way) were trying to get me to see back then. I'm not perfect by any means, but I've really tried to be intentional about moving differently. I'm even running for Junior Class Council president to make sure I'm doing my part.

That said, the catalyst for this letter: A couple nights ago the world learned that colleges are no longer allowed to consider race in their admissions processes. Now, I'll be brutally honest with you, which feels like a safe thing to do here in these letters no one else will read. (Which is maybe why Justyce told me to write them? Interesting . . .)

Anyway: When the news came in, and Justyce first told me? Well, it didn't hit me the way it hit him. Old me didn't surface completely, but I had a moment where I remembered how I felt when I learned Justyce had been accepted but I got deferred. Since we WERE equally qualified, no one can tell me Affirmative Action hadn't played a role in all that. So hearing about the Supreme Court's decision to change the rules initially gave me this burst of validation.

Which was uncomfortable. Especially when walking around campus and seeing how people from different racial groups were reacting to the news. It's like there were small, dark clouds floating over the heads of all the students who aren't white.

Then two things happened:

1. In my Constitutional Law class, our professor announced that for our final project, we'll be partnered with someone from the other class section "to create a presidential campaign where your proposed policies are rooted in opposing positions to your personal beliefs." Aka, we'll have to work with a stranger to convince our professor that we believe the opposite of what we put on the "Personal Politics" survey she made us fill out on the first day of class. I'm sure this doesn't sound like THAT big a deal, but considering there was a point where I DID believe the

opposite of what I do now, I'm scared of reopening the Pandora's box of that antiquated viewpoint . . . especially with someone I don't know.

And then:

2. I went to a second meeting for this election process and learned that the rules say you can't run if you have any sort of criminal record.

Under normal circumstances, this prohibition would've gone "in one ear and out the other," as your dad used to put it when we weren't engaged in active listening (the good ol' days!). After all, I don't have a criminal record.

Except . . . Well, I _should_ have one, is the thing. I got a DUI last year. The only reason it DIDN'T go on my record is because my dad got his lawyers involved.

Now I know the SEEMINGLY "right" thing to do is to rescind my intention to run. In fact, if people found out that I got an underage DUI but can still run for president because of a technicality, but our school's star running back (a Black guy) got EXPELLED for an underage DUI despite his BAC being _below_ the legal limit, also because of a technicality . . .

Yeah, that wouldn't be a good look for me.

However, if I DO pull out of the race, my sole opponent—who's a real piece of work, lemme tell ya—will automatically become JCC president. And as HE would like nothing more than to toss the campus back into the early 1800s, allowing him to run unopposed genuinely feels irresponsible.

Case in point: The idiot strolled into the second meeting late and entitled, fresh from baseball practice and reeking of week-old jock strap juice and "outside." (I used to love when your mom said that.) Q&A time rolled around, and this guy STOOD UP and said, "Since it's clearly not going to be addressed by the current administration of this so-called 'student-led organization,' I will be courageous enough to point out that the end of Affirmative Action is going to mean some pretty big changes around here."

The prez cut him off with a reminder that "barring direct relevance to THIS organization, no other topics need to be discussed," but, of course, Juice-Pouch LeDingaling the Freak (aka John Preston LePlante IV) didn't like that very much. His commentary isn't worthy of being written down, but let's just say he has this way of dismissing anyone who disagrees with him, with condescension so thick, you can feel it on your skin. Jackass almost started a brawl.

And I'm supposed to let HIM win?

It's quite the dilemma. And I don't have a ton of time to think on it: The declaration of candidacy is due at midnight tomorrow.

I just . . . How do I do "the right thing" when BOTH things could be considered "right"? All depends on how you look at them, doesn't it?

I gotta run because we have a house meeting at my fraternity (which I kinda hate being a part of, but we can save that for another letter). I'll reach out again soon, I guess.

That felt weird to write, but there it is.

Sincerely,

Jared

P.S. In other things that feel weird to write: I miss you, man. Like . . . a lot. Really wish you were here.

3

Divided We Fall

11:52 p.m. That's the time Jared gets his candidacy stuff turned in online.

(Because of course he went through with it. How could he not?)

Getting everything ready was tough. Jared, Justyce, and Amir Tsarfati—Jared's Moroccan American roommate from freshman year who'd agreed to be his campaign manager—spent *hours* working and reworking Jared's candidacy statement. Jared smiled as he read the campaign slogan they came up with (Ever Forward!), and even felt a small swell of pride as he tapped the submit button in the candidate registration portal.

Good feeling didn't last, though. Because the confirmation page included a link. And when he clicked on *that,* up popped the list of people who'd registered to run for Junior Class Council president . . .

There were *three* of them.

Jared Christensen
John Preston LePlante IV
Dylan M. Coleman

Who the hell is Dylan M. Coleman?

Jared grabs his phone and does a quick search on the first social media app that comes to mind. But there are far too many "Dylan Coleman" accounts to try to wade through. His fingertips tingle as he eyeballs the browser's search bar. Any normal person would just look up the name on the internet. But Jared . . . can't. He's too scarred from the media bias incidents senior year that framed Manny and Justyce as menaces to society who essentially got what was coming to them when they were shot by an off-duty police officer. For months after, anyone who searched his friends' names got fed a bunch of lies.

Jared hasn't been able to look up any not-famous person since. So the question runs through his head on a loop all night.

What he knows for sure: He did *not* see the name Dylan M. Coleman on the sign-in sheets at either of the mandatory UCC pre-candidacy meetings. Is it possible the guy came in after Jared was seated, like Jiggly Puffton LePuny always did? Yes.

But still: Jared P. Christensen does not like this curveball. Not one little bit.

When he gets to Constitutional Law—which is set up "grounded seminar style," aka beanbag chairs arranged in a circle—John Preston is already there. Kicked back in his chosen pouf with his hands clasped behind his head and his eyes closed like he doesn't have a care in the world. Jared feels a surge of anger that he *knows* is irrational—how the hell is John Preston so friggin *calm*? But it compels him forward. He lets his bag fall to the floor with a thud, and then drops down into the beanbag on John Preston's right with the force of an exasperated elephant.

The guy doesn't even flinch.

Jared rolls his eyes. "Hey, LePlante—"

"Shhh," from John Preston. "I'm meditating."

"Dude, whatever. Did you see there's a third candidate in the race?"

"Yep." He still hasn't moved. Or opened his eyes. It's unnerving.

"Well, do you know anything about him? I don't think he was at any meetings—"

"You sound mighty worried, Christensen."

"I'm not *worried*. I just—"

But Jared *is* worried. So worried, he doesn't realize the classroom has filled, and Dr. Yeh is settling into her own beanbag. As they take what she calls a grounding breath—everyone inhaling, "holding at the top," and exhaling collectively (*This class is so damn weird,* Jared thinks, even though he's supposed to be "emptying his mind")—Jared can feel how fast his heart is beating. His eyes lock on the closed classroom door, and it takes everything in him to keep from making a run for it.

He is so not in the headspace for one of Dr. Yeh's perspective-challenging class discussions.

But alas.

Dr. Phoebe Yeh: [*54, Chinese American, poli sci dept. chair.*] Class, class . . .

Everyone: Yes, yes!

Dr. Yeh: Fabulous. It's been said that the U.S. Constitution is a "living document." Can someone tell me what that means?

Everyone: [. . .]

Dr. Yeh: [*Smiles.*] We need some encouragement today, I see. Fine. Mr. Hardison . . . What say you?

Dionte Hardison: [*19, African American, star wide receiver and literal genius.*] To *me,* it means the document isn't static. It's gotta be reinterpreted over time as language shifts and standards change.

Amir Tsarfati: [*20, Moroccan American, Jared's campaign manager.*] This guy literally never misses.

Dr. Yeh: Correct. It's why I called on him.

Everyone: [*Laughs.*]

Dr. Yeh: Your turn, though, Mr. Tsarfati. Whose job is it to reinterpret the Constitution for the shaping of legislation over time?

Amir: The U.S. Supreme Court.

Dr. Yeh: And how does this continual reinterpretation come about?

Amir: Through cases that've been ruled on by lower courts but are being appealed. You gotta hit me harder than that, Doc.

Dr. Yeh: [*Smirks.*] Challenge accepted, young man.

Ainsley Cruz: [*19, biracial white Cuban/white American, Jared's ex-girlfriend.*] Ooh, this is getting juicy!

Jared: [*Rolls eyes.*]

Dr. Yeh: How is the U.S. Supreme Court formed, Mr. Tsarfati?

Amir: Well, it's been a lifetime-appointed gig since its founding—

Imani Williams: [*20, African American, third-generation legacy student.*] Unless a justice gets impeached—

John Preston: Which has only happened one time, and the guy was acquitted.

Dr. Yeh: All correct. Please continue, Mr. Tsarfati.

Amir: Well, when an active justice dies or retires and there's a vacancy, the sitting president nominates someone, and the Senate votes to confirm that person by simple majority.

Dr. Yeh: Meaning?

Amir: As long as more senators vote FOR the confirmation than against it, the nominee becomes the new justice.

Dr. Yeh: And what is the role of the general public in all this?

Amir: [*Smug smile vanishes.*] Uhh . . .

Dr. Yeh: What's that you kids say? *Got eeeem?*

Everyone: [*Laughs.*]

Dr. Yeh: Mr. Christensen?

Jared: [*Startled.*] Huh?

John Preston: [*Snorts.*]

Dr. Yeh: I believe you know the answer to my question: Considering the process for selecting and confirming Supreme Court justices, what is the role of the general public in how the U.S. Constitution is continually reinterpreted for the creation of new laws?

Jared: [. . .]

Everyone: [. . .]

Jared: Well—

John Preston: [*Butting in as usual.*] The role of—

Dr. Yeh: I was speaking to Mr. Christensen, Mr. LePlante.

Imani: Oop!

Jared: [*Sits up straighter.*] As I was saying, the general public elects the president—

John Preston: Through the electoral college—

Ainsley: You should really stop cutting him off, JP. It's making you look a little thirsty.

Amir: Double oop!

Everyone: [*Laughs.*]

Dr. Yeh: A grounding breath, please.

Everyone: [*Breathes.*]

Dr. Yeh: You were saying, Mr. Christensen?

Jared: Both the person who nominates a new justice and the people who vote to confirm are elected by the general public. The president through the electoral college, yes. But senators are elected by popular vote.

Dr. Yeh: [*Smiles.*]

Amir: Which shows how important it is to choose our representatives well. Jared Christensen for JCC president!

Jared: [*Smacks his forehead.*]

Dr. Yeh: [*Very much half-heartedly . . . and still smiling.*] That's enough, Mr. Tsarfati.

Amir hits Jared with a wink and a finger gun, and though Jared shakes his head, he can't help but smile too. It's a nice reprieve from the storm in his mind, and he had no idea how good it would feel to receive Dr. Yeh's silent approval, even if her class makes his brain hurt.

He feels significantly lighter as they draw to a close and manages to stay on chill as Dr. Yeh reminds them about their big project.

"Your partner assignments are posted outside the door," she says after dismissing everyone. "My suggestion is to get acquainted as soon as possible."

As he's walking out, Ainsley approaches him to say how smart she thinks he is and that he's got her vote (wild considering he dumped her last semester), and Dionte Hardison, who Jared thinks is cooler than a polar bear's butt, lifts his chin and smiles, which . . . was that approval? Had to be, right?

He's feeling *good*—

But just like last night, it doesn't last. Because when he scans the partner list and sees who he's with, Jared's high spirits come crashing back to earth with the force of the meteor that killed the dinosaurs.

There beside *Jared Christensen* are the words "Dylan M. Coleman."

He looks back inside the classroom.

Dr. Yeh is still smiling at him.

4

A More Perfect Union

The email landed in Jared's school account around 8:30 that same evening:

> Hello, Jared.
>
> This is Dylan Coleman, your assigned partner for the Constitutional Law final project. As the assignment looks to be fairly labor-intensive based on the project description and rubric Dr. Yeh sent out, and I'm certain we both have other obligations vying for our time and attention, I hope you'll be amenable to getting a jump on things.
>
> I'm available tomorrow afternoon at 2 p.m. and can meet you at Common Grounds café—you're

familiar, I presume? It's located just south of
campus in Old Downtown. My suggestion is that
we spend an hour learning about one another's
political leanings, mining our commonalities,
and determining our shared goals so that we
can decide on the best direction to take for this
project and the most efficient and effective means
of achieving our objectives.

I await your response and look forward to making
your acquaintance.

Best,
Dylan M. Coleman

He'd gone through it three times, his discomfort intensifying
with each reread. It was very formal, yes, but Jared knew that any
professor would consider it well written. (This was annoying.) He
also knew that being partnered with this guy suggested their political leanings were similar. Which made him even more nervous
about the election.

But speaking of the election: Jared didn't know what to make
of ol' Dylan not mentioning it at all. Did the guy not know he'd
been partnered with a political opponent? Or was it some sort of
trick?

The latter possibility is kicking around in his mind as Jared
approaches Common Grounds café the following afternoon. His
phone buzzes in his pocket, and he pulls it out: Amir letting him
know his campaign team is officially at twenty-seven members.
Aka three short of the maximum allowed.

He smiles. *Take* that, *Dylan M. Coleman.*

He walks in at 2:01 p.m. and looks around, hoping against hope that this guy knows what Jared looks like. There are people everywhere.

After a couple minutes with no one waving him over, Jared approaches the counter to place an order—anything to keep from continuing to stand there, looking lost—and decides to use the phone number included in the last email. He taps out a text:

> I'm here. Grabbing a sandwich and drink. You want anything?

He waits a bit for a reply but doesn't get one, so he slides his phone back into his pocket. The possibility that he's being tricked pops into his head, and he clenches and releases his jaw as he takes another look around the space.

He sees a couple making goo-goo eyes at each other over what he suspects are drinks that have matching latte art. (Gross.) A trio of sorority girls appear to be arguing over something on one of their computer screens. (Typical.) And there's also a pair of nerdy dudes at a shared table who are so focused on *their* computer screens and typing with such ferocity, it wouldn't surprise Jared to learn they're having some sorta coding contest.

Most of the tables, though, have a single occupant with an open laptop or textbook. Multiple brunettes in "athleisure" with messy top knots, a premed student here, a philosophy one over there. And at the table where Jared would typically sit, tucked back into a corner where he can people watch, there's a cute Black girl—one of only two Black people in the whole café. (Gotta love Connecticut.)

The only person Jared recognizes is a dude from Biology 101, and when the kid shoves his glasses up higher on his face and then picks his nose, Jared shudders.

He checks his phone again before stepping up to the counter. Still nothing from his project partner. "Ooh, you're cute!" the barista says.

Jared can't muster the juice to flirt back, even though she's cute too . . . light-brown skin, dark eyes, long, straight black hair. He's clearly been influenced by SJ Friedman: There was a time when he wouldn't have even *noticed* that the girl has a different skin tone than him, let alone other features that "code" as South Asian.

"Wow, clearly barking up the wrong tree," she says when he doesn't reply. Jared opens his mouth to say *something* but realizes it's futile. She won't even look at him now. "What can I get you?"

"I'll take a sausage, egg, and cheese croissant and a medium peppermint tea with agave syr—"

"Christensen! That you, bro?"

Jared turns around, and a sigh of relief whooshes out of him. Approaching are a quartet of other white guys he plays intramural basketball with and genuinely likes: Pat Neuman, a guy from the Atlanta Metro area (Jared called him out for saying he's "from Atlanta" when he grew up in burby Peachtree Corners); Robbie and Roger Range, a set of fraternal twins from Baton Rouge; and Aaron Karo, a Jewish dude from California and the only one of the five who actually plays for their collegiate team.

"My GUY!" Robbie says, wrapping Jared in a bear hug. The Range twins are big huggers.

Jared groans. (The guy is six foot three and 220 pounds of lean muscle.) "Great to see you too, Rob."

"Yo, when are we getting this campaign shit poppin', my friend?" from Aaron.

"Campaign?" Pat asks. "What campaign?"

"Our guy's a presidential candidate!" Robbie replies. "You didn't know?"

It hits Jared. "Wait, are you guys on my campaign team?"

"Are we *on* your *campaign team*?" Aaron again. "*Really,* man? What are you even *asking*? Of *course* we're on your campaign team!" (So *passionate,* this guy.)

"*I'm* not on the campaign team." Pat is appalled. "How are these assholes on the campaign team, but I'm not? That's how you're gonna do your boy, Christensen?"

Jared raises his hands. "Whoa now, *I* didn't even know they were on the campaign team." He turns to Roger, the most sensible of the bunch. "Amir put you on?"

"Yeah," Roger says. "We're looking forward to helping you bring home that victory, Mr. President." Roger throws an arm around Jared's shoulders and pulls him in for an *I Believe in You* squeeze. (See? Huggers.)

"When do we get to learn more about our platform?" Aaron says.

"No, man." Pat puts a hand up. "Can't go there yet. I would like to be on the campaign team, please and thank you. Who do I need to contact?"

Jared smiles. The overt and unabashed support from dudes who look like him feels good. Especially since he knows these guys have similar worldviews: Pat is one of those students who can't resist going to school year-round, and Jared knows he does his summer semesters at Morehouse, a historically Black college in Atlanta.

Roger and Robbie are utterly loaded, but their parents sent them to racially diverse public schools pre-k through high school graduation. And then there's Aaron, who is basically the basketball-playing dude version of SJ Friedman. He's Jewish and prelaw with a focus on civil rights, like Jared. In fact, he's the person who taught Jared that "civil" rights means the rights of *citizens.*

"I'd be honored to have you join, Pat," Jared says. "I'll put you in contact with Amir. My officer candidate meeting is in a few days, and we'll gather after that and go over all the info before campaigns go live next week."

Pat nods. "Word."

Jared's food and drink come up, and he finds a table and goes to sit.

Soon all the fellas have joined him. "Man, you guys showed up at just the right time," he says, biting into his sandwich.

"Oh yeah?" Roger replies. "What's going on?"

Jared sighs. "Any of you taking Constitutional Law with Dr. Yeh?"

They all shake their heads.

"Well, count yourselves blessed. She's an awesome professor, but we have this monster of a final project, and *she* chose our partners for it. Mine was supposed to meet me here"—he checks his watch—"sixteen minutes ago. A meeting *he* set. But the bastard stood me up."

"Dang," Roger says. "I'm sorry, dude."

Jared glowers, fully in his feelings now. "Gets worse. Apparently this guy is also running against me. So not only is he clearly unreliable—which doesn't bode well for *my* workload on a two-person project worth twenty-five percent of my grade—but I also have to work with a literal political opponent. I'm pretty sure the professor set me up—"

"Excuse me . . ." A silky voice cuts Jared's tirade. He looks up . . . and stops breathing. There standing over him is the Black girl who was at his usual corner table. Up close—and with his mind on nothing else considering how off guard she caught him—Jared can't help but be struck by . . . how nice she is to look at. He can see her figure in his peripheral vision and . . . yeah.

He would *never* say it aloud—no white boy in his right mind wants to be accused of thinking all Black people look alike. But she reminds him of Liberty Ayers, a girl—well, *woman,* really—he met last year while working with Justyce to help Manny's cousin with some legal stuff. This girl's skin is a rich brown and super glowy, and she's got a tiny hoop through one nostril, just like Liberty did.

The main difference is her hair. Where Liberty had locs (Jared will never forget telling Liberty he liked her "dreadlocks" and getting pierced through to his very soul with a look of death as she said "Never attach the word *dread* to hair like mine again"), this girl has straight, silky black hair that hangs to her lower back.

"It's a wig," she says.

"Huh?" Because what the hell else is Jared supposed to say to that?

"You're staring at my hair. It's a wig."

"Oh . . . okay . . ." Jared breaks the eye contact and looks around at his friends. They're all just staring at her. Robbie and Pat both have their mouths open.

She shakes her head and crosses her arms. "I bet you don't even remember me."

Panic floods Jared's chest. Because she's right—he doesn't.

"*You're* the guy who almost knocked me over in the poli-sci building last week," she says. "*My bad . . .*" She rolls her eyes and mocks what Jared guesses is supposed to be his voice, and the memory of rushing out after that initial UCC meeting kicks him in the brain. Jared floods with shame.

"Not that *you* would know it, but I dropped all my books."

Jared's eyes zip around to all his friends. They're still staring at her. "Uhhh . . . I'm sorry?" is all he can muster.

"You're Jared Christensen, right?"

Oh god, she knows his name? "Yes?"

She smirks. "You asking me or telling me?"

"Huh?"

"You don't sound very sure about that being who you are."

Jared doesn't respond to that. (Can't.)

She looks him over in a way that makes his face even hotter. "You're actually kinda cute," she says. "Which is annoying. Anyway . . ." The girl sticks her hand out. Before Jared can register the movement, he feels her warm palm against his clammy one. Her fragrance crashes over him.

"Dylan Marie Coleman," she says, giving their joined hands a good pump. "Pleasure to make your acquaintance, Mr. Christensen."

5

United We Stand

Jared's plan seemed simple enough: Drag Amir to the officer candidate meeting and use him as a buffer. The guy *is* his campaign manager, after all, and Jared scoured the UCC election guidelines for rules prohibiting a candidate from bringing a plus-one to a meeting. He couldn't find any.

Is it risky? Maybe. But one: Dylan, without explanation, canceled the third project meeting they were supposed to have yesterday. And Jared hasn't spoken to her since, so he has no idea what she'll be like when he sees her today. And two: The idea of being in the same room as political opponent "Dylan M. Coleman"—whom he feels like he still hasn't met, despite *two* meetings so far with her alter ego, project partner Dylan Marie Coleman—without moral support was . . . He couldn't even bring himself to think about it.

Is it odd that there have been zero mentions of the election in their conversations? Of course it is. But she hasn't brought it up, so Jared hasn't either. He clearly won't be able to ignore it *this* evening, though. He and Amir even arrive fifteen minutes early so they can sit close to the front—needs to be clear that he means business.

What Jared doesn't count on is Dylan wafting in like a rose petal caught on a gentle breeze. Nor does he expect her to settle her glorious self into the empty seat on the other side of him. (When he thinks about it later, he'll realize how John Preston LePlante it was of her.)

A cute East Asian girl sits on Dylan's other side, and before Jared can open his mouth to speak, *that* girl has leaned forward and stuck out her hand. "You must be Jared," she says. "Avis Johnson. Spelled like the rental car company but sounds like 'Travis.' I'm Dyl's campaign manager. Pleasure to make your acquaintance."

"Ah." Jared's hand engulfs Avis's smaller one. "Yeah, I'm Jared—"

"And I'm Amir," Amir says, knocking Jared's arm away and taking Avis's hand in his own. "Amir Tsarfati. *His* campaign manager. I'd say it's a pleasure to make *your* acquaintance, Ms. . . . Johnson, did you say? But I'm not sure about that yet."

"Dude." Jared covers his face.

Dylan snorts but doesn't say a word.

"Did you bring an *entourage,* Christensen?" comes a voice from behind them that makes Jared feel like his flesh is shriveling. "Who do you think you are, P. Diddy?"

"Wow, *someone* clearly doesn't listen to actual hip-hop or keep up with current events," Dylan says. "That reference is so late-'90s and deeply problematic, it's appalling."

"Meet John Preston LePlante the fourth," Jared says without turning around.

"Oh, I know who he is." Dyl rotates to address their shared opponent directly. "Your reputation for unwarranted arrogance precedes you," she says. "Have there really been *four* of you? God help us all."

"*Excuse* me?" John Preston replies.

"Truly wish I could, trust."

"Damn, homegirl doesn't play around," Amir whispers to Jared.

John Preston to Dylan: "Bro, who even *are* you?"

"Oh, I'm *your* worst nightmare, sweetie," she says. "Have a seat, though, yeah? Meeting's starting."

Jared tries to focus. He really does. Especially after hearing "Dyl" eat John Preston like a handful of Flavor Blasted Goldfish. But something else he wouldn't have counted on: how comforting her presence turns out to be. Can't put it into words because he's never experienced anything like it, but he spends the meeting more relaxed than he's been since his best friend was killed two years prior.

It's disconcerting, this seeming sorcery. But it feels so good *not* to be wound up, Jared can't find it in himself to resist. His sole moment of tension comes during the Q&A. And of course it's catalyzed by Jerkish Prickton LePoop the Fart:

John Preston: Thank you for that illuminating presentation, Miss . . . Park, is it?

Ari: As this is the third meeting I've presided over, I would hope you know my name by now.

John Preston: Fair enough. You mentioned "DEI." Can you explain what you mean by that?

Ari: Diversity, equity, and inclusion. All concepts prioritized by this organization.

John Preston: Ah, I see. I thought those letters stood for *Didn't Earn It.*

Ari: Come again?

Jared feels Dylan rise to her feet beside him, and his pulse speeds up.

Dylan: Sincerest apologies for interjecting, Ms. President. But I'd like to say something, if it's okay with you?

Ari: By all means.

Dylan: Thank you. Though I presume the previous comment was a tasteless attempt at a joke, as an African American female student, I would like to express *my* appreciation for the UCC's prioritization of diversity, equity, and inclusion. I would also like to point out that acquiring wealth through the cultivation, by enslaved Black people, of land stolen from Indigenous people—all while suppressing the political and economic advancement of women, banning and penalizing the immigration of Asian people, and stigmatizing the very existence of Latino people—and *then* holding on to that wealth through intergenerational nepotism, legislative bullying, and the exploitation of poor people? THAT is the *epitome* of "didn't earn it," as my opponent so ineloquently put it. Thank you.

Ari: *(failing to suppress her smile)* Meeting's adjourned.

To Jared's complete surprise, John Preston doesn't say a word. Just grabs his bag and storms out. And despite it not being his *own* victory, Jared doesn't think he's ever felt more satisfied.

The foursome exits the room single file: first Avis, then Dylan, then Jared, and then Amir. Once they're in the hallway, Dylan spins to face Jared, and he stumbles back a step to keep from crashing into her. Which means Amir crashes into him.

"Whoa," Jared says.

"Wanna ditch these minions and go work on the project?" from Dylan.

"Umm, excuse you," Avis says.

"Yeah," from Amir. "That was below the belt. Also, at least have the decency to shake a guy's hand and exchange pleasantries before insult—"

"I mean, you did kinda blow me off yesterday," Jared says, shocking himself with the forwardness. "We're definitely behind now. I'd say you owe me *and* our grade the courtesy."

They lock into intense (and maybe a little competitive?) eye contact, and for the span of a few beats, it's like everything and everyone else has ceased to exist. Jared hates to admit it, but he totally understands John Preston's question: Who even *is* this girl? (Young lady? Woman? What is *happening*?)

"Guess that's *our* cue to leave," Avis says, shattering the moment and knocking Jared right back to reality. What the hell is he doing, flirting with his opponent?

"You said it, not me," Dylan says to Avis without taking her eyes off Jared.

Avis: "Disgusting."

Amir: "And appalling."

Avis: "I mean, the nerve—"

"Student center?" Dylan continues to Jared, cutting Avis off.

"After you, madam."

Jared cringes at his response, but she walks off, so he follows her.

"Well, you're both welcome for our support!" he hears Amir say as they go.

6

Blessings of Liberty

When Jared and Dylan arrive at said student center—after a charged five-minute walk across campus where their hands kept brushing—it's packed.

And Dylan Marie Coleman apparently doesn't do crowds.

"Is there somewhere else we can go?" she asks, rotating to face him. "With fewer people? Sorry, I still don't know this campus super well."

That gets Jared's attention. "Huh?"

"I just transferred here," she replies. "Started at the beginning of the semester."

Questions begin to roll in Jared's head like the opening of a Star Wars film: *From where? Why in the middle of the year? Are transfer students allowed to run for office? Does she know enough about this school to even run? Does she actually like it here?* But the look on her face makes it clear this isn't the time to ask.

Thus, they wind up somewhere he would've never anticipated: at the door to his apartment.

Everything that follows feels like a scene from a reality-TV dating show.

INTERIOR: Hallway outside door to El Manor McAlliChristensen

Having reached their destination, Dylan turns to look Jared in the eye.

DYLAN

You trying to get in my pants, Christensen?

JARED

What? No! Of course not.

Dylan's eyes narrow.

DYLAN

You swear it? I Googled the shit outta you and saw some impressive things, but I also don't know you like that, and I really don't wanna have to kick your ass.

Dylan looks Jared up and down. Jared, fighting the urge to ask what she found on him, raises one hand and puts the other one over his heart.

JARED

I swear it on my honor.

Dylan moves aside, and Jared gets the door
open. They enter, and Dylan takes in the
space as they head to the living room. Once
at the couch, she drops her bag, they sit,
and it's straight to business.

DYLAN

Okay, where'd we leave off at our last
meet— Oh my god, this couch is a comfort
trap. How dare you bring me here?

JARED
(laughing)

Sorry, should've warned you. My mom
picked it. She has this thing about
the living room being "a home's most
welcoming space." You totally didn't ask
for all that, but yeah.

DYLAN
(shrugging)

Nice little insight into my partner's
life. Thanks for sharing.

There's a moment of charged eye contact, but
Dylan is quick to break it. She claps and

reaches to pull a notebook and pen out of
her bag.

DYLAN

Anyway, let's get to this project, shall
we? What'd we last talk about?

JARED
*(scrambling to get his laptop out
and open)*

Uhhh . . . Looks like we were trying to
figure out if there are any areas where
we disagree politically.

DYLAN
Ah, yes. And on abortion rights, race
relations, diversity and equity initiatives,
public education policy, and student debt
forgiveness, we agreed completely.

JARED
(blushing, but not knowing why)

Right.

DYLAN

Which leaves climate change, the economy,
America's role in world affairs, and
criminal justice and policing to hash out.

Jared gulps.

DYLAN

Where should we start?

JARED

(gulping again)

What's the assignment again?

DYLAN

(paraphrasing from her screen)

We have to choose five contemporary
issues and design a political campaign
where our imaginary candidate holds the
opposite beliefs from ours.

JARED

I swear she's trying to kill us.

DYLAN

Yep. So climate change. Thoughts?

Jared takes an ultra-low-key deep breath.

JARED

I mean, the climate has obviously
changed. . . . And if you believe
science—which I do—it's primarily because
of actions humans have taken.

DYLAN

Okay . . . and what should be done about
that?

JARED

I think if we broke it, we gotta fix it.
There are those giant carbon vacuums.
And I was reading last week about this
company trying to cultivate a type of
seaweed that sucks up carbon and contains
it.

Dylan draws back, looking confused.

DYLAN

Why were you reading about this?

JARED
(turning red)

I get a daily *Washington Post*
e-newsletter that highlights seven news
stories every morning. It . . . uhh . . .
might be the first thing I read when I
wake up?

DYLAN
(smiling and nudging Jared with an
elbow)

You asking me or telling me?

JARED

Well played, Coleman.

DYLAN

Oh god, don't call me that.

She shudders but doesn't explain.

DYLAN

Anyway, we're aligned on climate change.
Let's do criminal justice and policing.
Do you think the police should be
defunded and/or abolished?

JARED
*(trying not to pass out or feign a
medical emergency)*

Mmmm . . . I mean, no? I get *why* there
are people who push for that, but I don't
think it's the smartest thing to do.
At least not until a better system has
been designed, tested, and proven more
effective.

There's a loooooong pause.

DYLAN

I hear that. My favorite uncle is a cop
in Virginia, and he and I frequently talk
about it. He's lost a lot of friends over
the years, and even some of our family

members cut ties with him after those
five Black cops in Memphis beat that
Black skateboarder to death. But Unc also
rescued six kids from the pickup truck
of a registered sex offender during a
traffic stop. He sees it as his duty to
be one of the good ones until we figure
out something better.

JARED

My best friend was killed by a cop.

Beat as the words land.

He didn't even do anything wrong.

DYLAN
(*nodding*)

Yeah. I read about it. Emmanuel Rivers,
right?

Jared doesn't know what to say.

DYLAN

When I saw that Dr. Yeh made us partners,
I looked you up. Found an old newsclip
where you were speaking out against the
way your friends were being portrayed in
the media after being shot.

JARED

Oh.

DYLAN

Also found an article about you, a Black
guy, and a white girl working to get a
wrongfully incarcerated kid released
from jail. I was actually pretty excited
to work with you . . . until I found a
picture and saw you were the asshole who
knocked all my stuff out of my hands and
kept going.

JARED

You're never gonna let me live that down,
huh?

DYLAN

That is correct. Even though you've been
quite the gentleman since. I'm sorry
about what happened to your friends.

They lapse into silence, and Jared's palms
begin to itch. He is suddenly overcome with
the urge to say more than he knows he should.
He's not sure what it is, but something about
Dylan makes her far too easy to talk to. . . .

JARED

You know why that question was hard for
me to answer?

Beat as he realizes what he's doing . . . and does it anyway.

JARED

I've benefited. From the unfair treatment. I got an underage DUI last year, but it's not even on my record. My dad "didn't want my future ruined," so he had his lawyers work to get it scrubbed.

Dylan stays quiet and blank-faced. Jared knows he should stop talking, but he can't seem to.

JARED

And like I'm obviously thankful. Can't think of anyone who would *want* their future ruined. But it messes with me to this day because I *know* that if I'd been a Black guy, things likely would've gone very differently—

DYLAN

Like they're going for that football player.

Jared opens his mouth and then lets it shut. The air seems to thicken.

JARED

I mean—

Peppy jazz fills the room, and Dylan jumps.
It's her phone. She pulls it from her pocket
and looks at the screen. Her eyes go wide,
and she leaps to her feet.

DYLAN
(scrambling to gather her things)

I'm so sorry, but I have to take this.

Before Jared can respond, the front door is
shutting behind her.

Cut to black.

April 10

Dear Manny,

Honestly wasn't expecting to write again at all, let alone what feels like so soon, but things have gotten _weird_, and I have NO IDEA what to do about any of it.

The long and short of it: There's a girl. Well . . . there are two girls, really, though one is only relevant here because of the other one (respectfully). The more important one is named Dylan Marie Coleman. She's my partner on that project I mentioned in my first letter, and she's also running against me in this presidential race. (Side note: Pretty sure Dr. Yeh set me up. Found out she's the faculty advisor for the UCC.)

A few nights ago, Dylan fled my apartment like a thief in the night. And she hasn't responded to any of my check-in messages. And like, fine: I did start to freak out a TINY bit. I shared something I maybe shouldn't have just before she left. But there's also been a lot going on—like the campaigns launched yesterday morning—so I haven't really had time to think too much about any of it.

However: The past three hours have thrown my cool, calm, and collected into a blender. Started with an email from her inviting me to collaborate on a shared document that turned out to be a proposed outline for our project. Like . . . impeccably detailed and with an explanation for each issue she chose.

Did it bother me that she'd done all this work but left my messages on read? Yeah. A little bit.

But whatever. If she was gonna put some work in, so could I. I went for a run to clear my head, then went to the library.

And everything would've been perfectly fine had I not been passing by the student center right as she came out of it. She was with some other people, most of them students of color. (One of them, Dionte Hardison, is actually in MY section of Constitutional Law.) But the sight of HER? Bro, I dunno what came over me, but I wanted to run over, literally scoop her up, and carry her away so she'd never leave my sight again. Which is something I have no idea how to explain.

It might be THE creepiest thing I've ever felt in my life, but there you have it.

I picked up my pace in hopes of orchestrating a "Whoa, fancy meeting you here!" encounter, except ten yards or so away, I heard my name called. . . .

And so did she. Her chin lifted, and we shared a moment of eye contact before she gave me a (very enticing) half smile and lifted her chin in greeting. Totally gave me a little thrill . . .

But whatever vaguely confusing delight I was feeling got samurai-sword sliced clean down the middle when the person who called me stepped into my path, bouncing on the toes of her impractical shoes as though there were springs in the high-ass heels.

Enter girl number two: Ainsley Michelle Cruz. Henceforth known as the Ex.

Quickest backstory ever: My dad and the Ex's dad are alums and former roommates, and they'd like nothing more than for the Ex and me to get married and make them some little Bulldog grandbabies (that's our school's mascot). And I tried to lean into it, Manny. I really did. For like a semester and a half last year. Ainsley is quite the hot commodity around campus, and she really is a very sweet and very smart girl (when she lets it show). I'm just . . . not into her, you know?

Anyway, so she's standing there beaming up at me like I'M the one who painted the sky the same color as her eyes. (They're nice, her eyes . . . but still.) "Thought that was you, stud muffin!" she said. (I had to fight not to roll MY eyes.) I reluctantly wrapped a single arm around her waist as she threw both of hers around my neck and pressed her full body against me, but my gaze drifted back to Dylan.

Who was watching me. She wiggled her eyebrows and gave me a look of teasing approval.

Couldn't have hated it more.

"I'm really glad I ran into you!" the Ex said, regrabbing my attention. "My dad is coming to town to see a client this weekend, and he wants to take us to dinner." (It should be noted that neither Ainsley nor either of our fathers have accepted that she and I are broken up.) "I was going to text you about it this afternoon, but getting to ask in person is—"

And I didn't hear a word she said beyond that because the sound of the word "text" shifted my focus right back to Dylan. Who was still watching me. We locked eyes again.

I heard the Ex say "What are you staring at?" a hair too late, and before I could stop her, she was checking over her shoulder.

"Wait . . . isn't that the girl who is running against you in the presidential race?" She turned back to me. "Are you even serious right now?"

"Ains, relax." Not my finest moment in any universe, but all I could think about was her telling her dad—who would then tell MY dad—that I was making goo-goo eyes at a Black woman while the Ex was actively inviting me to dinner. "Yeah, she's running against me, but she's also my assigned partner for the Yeh project—"

"Which YOU clearly don't mind." She crossed her arms.

"Ains—"

"News flash, buddy: I'm a <u>woman</u>. We can tell when the guy we love is into someone else."

I knew there was no arguing at that point, Manny.

She glared over her shoulder again, and if the change in Dylan's expression was any indication, the Ex's eye lasers of death had reached their intended target.

"Just be careful, okay?" she continued, turning back to me. She swiped the tears from her face. "I've heard some things about that girl, and none of them are nice. Have fun with your 'project.'" She shoved past me and walked off.

It would've been fine, Manny. Like even if she did run and tattle to the dads, the whole thing could've been chalked up to her being upset about me moving on, and eventually things would've blown over. But when I got back to my apartment—there's no way I could concentrate after all that, so I skipped the library—I had a direct message on the only social media platform I use, from an account with no followers, no profile pic, and no posts:

Didn't know our big-shot school let felons run for president, but I guess this IS America . . .

And there was a link.

Normally, I wouldn't have opened it in a million years. But . . . well, I panicked. Because that thing I maybe shouldn't have told Dylan about was my DUI.

So, I tapped. And there in the palm of my hand appeared a pair of mug shots, one straight on and one in profile.

Of Dylan Marie Coleman.

Thus, I've landed here. Again, writing to my dead best friend because I have no idea what to think or how to feel.

I haven't done any digging because I'm a little too in shock, I guess? Like I <u>knew</u> I didn't know much about her, but I didn't KNOW how much I don't know. You know?

All I can think about is the fact that the person I panic-spilled my deepest, darkest secret to (well, second deepest darkest . . . the first is that I hooked up with Melo Taylor last summer while intoxicated at a party; please don't go to Justyce in a dream and tell him) isn't only a political rival . . . she's clearly got some secrets of her own.

Now I worry I won't be able to look at her without seeing her mug shot. And look at her, I must. For one: We have a project to do. Trying to accomplish that while avoiding the sight of her face would be really awkward. And for two: I mean . . . she's impossible <u>not</u> to look at.

Now I'm EXTRA nervous about her choosing "criminal justice and policing" as one of our core issues. What if SHE was wrongfully arrested? And now she knows that my record was (wrongfully) wiped clean?

Man, I hope this doesn't turn into a raging disaster.

I'm gonna go add some stuff to our project doc so she knows I didn't meet up with Ainsley. Why I want Dylan to know that—especially after what I just saw—I'm not sure. But here we are.

Really wish you were here, man.

—Jared

ACT II

Match ~~Made~~ Met

7

Establish Justice

Jared is so discombobulated the following morning, he barely makes it into Dr. Yeh's room before the door closes. "Nice of you to join us, Mr. Christensen!" she says with a wink as he eases past her.

"Sorry, Professor." He steps out of his shoes and deposits then in a cubby, then turns around. He really wanted to sit beside Dionte today. (Not that he'd be able to explain why.)

But it's a no-go.

In fact, as though the literal nightmares that kept him up most of the night weren't a salient-enough source of misery, the only available beanbag is between Ainsley and John Preston.

Because of course it is.

"You look tired," Ainsley says as he sits.

So she *is* speaking to him. He assumed (hoped) she wouldn't be.

Killer observation, Nancy Drew is what he wants to say, but he resists. It would hurt her feelings, and she hasn't done anything to warrant the blow. He just prays she doesn't mention Dylan. It would full-force shove him right over an unknown edge, and there's no telling what he would say or do in response.

Jared, of course, couldn't resist looking into the whole mugshot thing. In fact, the minute he shut his notebook of secret letters, he broke his own cardinal rule and launched into a full-fledged scour of the internet in search of an arrest record for one Dylan Marie Coleman.

After two hours, sixteen minutes, and a downright absurd fee that he put on his emergency credit card—he figured if Dad asks about it, he could say he heard a rumor about a political opponent and needed to get some proof of broken rules in case he lost the election (the guy would likely be *proud* of Jared's "proactiveness")—he found what he was looking for: two charges in Newport News, Virginia. A property damage misdemeanor and an "unlawful wounding" felony.

All night, his mind ping-ponged between (a) knowing that if Dylan *did* decide to expose his secret, he had everything he needed to hit her right back, and (b) grappling with what he'd discovered. Because *property damage*? And what the hell was "unlawful wounding"? Jared couldn't help but think there was a weapon involved.

On top of all that was the fact that some anonymous person had unearthed Dylan's mug shot and created a dummy profile seemingly for the sole purpose of sending it to Jared. Why would they do that? His brief interaction with Ainsley initially popped into his mind—was it a jealousy thing?—but he's pretty sure she wouldn't waste her time on something like this.

Also: Had Anonymous Person also sent it to LePlante? Or any of the UCC higher-ups? Jared had a hunch the answer was no. Which made the whole thing that much more disconcerting. And the strangest part: What he felt most strongly about the whole thing was a bizarre instinct to *protect* Dylan. Which gave him a flashback of the time SJ Friedman told him to "always self-check and make sure that" he wasn't "on some white-guy-swoops-in-and-saves-the-day bullshit." She was referring to his interest in civil rights law, but the advice feels fitting here.

"A grounding breath before we begin, please," Dr. Yeh says, drawing him back into the classroom. Which unlocks a different kind of dread. Under any other circumstances, Jared would be thrilled to get pulled from the chaos of his own mind . . . but he knows which class he's in.

Dr. Yeh: Class, class . . .

Everyone: Yes, yes!

Dr. Yeh: Welcome. Thank you all for being here today. This morning, I received an email from a student with a link to a news story about a nearby school district that recently elected to remove a dozen contemporary children's books—many beloved by students—from school shelves after a complaint from a parent. The student had two questions for *me* that I'd like to propose to *you:* Could this issue be appealed to the Supreme Court for the sake of outlawing book banning on a federal level? And on what constitutional grounds could it be argued?

John Preston: Say *what* now?

Dr. Yeh: Would someone like to reiterate the question for Mr. LePlante?

John Preston: No, I heard the question. I just think it's ridiculous.

Imani: You think *what* is ridiculous?

John Preston: The idea of the Supreme Court wasting time on something this trivial.

Jared: Surprise, surprise.

Dr. Yeh: Do you intend to support that perspective from a constitutional perspective, Mr. LePlante?

John Preston: The Constitution has nothing to do with it. Public schools are funded by taxpayers. If said taxpayers feel that what their kids are being taught is inaccurate or inappropriate, they're well within their rights to demand changes to the curriculum.

Imani: Does that apply to *all* taxpayers? Or just certain ones?

John Preston: Huh?

Imani: My parents, for instance, are tax-paying, law-abiding U.S. citizens who live in a state where there are laws limiting what can be taught about American Chattel Slavery *and* the well-documented history of racist terror enacted against Black people post-emancipation. These limitations create *sweeping* inaccuracies in what kids are taught about this country. Can *my* parents "demand" changes to the curriculum too?

Amir: Williams with the slam DUNK.

Dr. Yeh: Constitution-based cosigns only, Mr. Tsarfati.

Everyone: [*Laughs.*]

John Preston: I'm just saying: People send their kids to school so they can learn what they need to know to succeed in this country.

It's clearly been deemed that these so-called "books" that've been removed—

Jared: They are *literal* books, dude. Nothing "so-called" about them.

Dionte: Yeah, man. You do this thing sometimes where you try to delegitimize something because you've decided it's not worthy of being called what it literally IS. That tendency is a prime example of the problem here.

Dr. Yeh: Which is what, Mr. Hardison?

Dionte: This idea certain people have that *their* standards and ideals are correct and universal.

Jared: I totally agree.

John Preston: Whatever. My point is that if leaders at the district level decided these books should be removed, they clearly don't see them as necessary to educational success.

Ainsley: I actually kind of agree? Like why should little kids be forced to learn about things that don't apply to them? In fact, why should *anyone* who's paying to get educated?

Jared: [*Can feel things headed somewhere they don't need to go . . .*]

Imani: What do you mean?

Ainsley: Well . . . I happened to be looking at the campaign statements for the Junior Class Council presidential nominees, and Dylan Coleman wants our school to implement an ethnic studies course requirement for all undergraduates.

Imani: Aaaand . . . that's a problem?

Ainsley: I mean, it's not a *problem.* I just don't see how any of the ethnic studies classes are relevant to our general education.

Imani: To *your* specific education, you mean.

Amir: [*To Ainsley.*] Why do we get stuffed with European history in high school? We're not in Europe.

Ainsley: I mean, this country was founded by Europeans—

Imani: But BUILT by Africans—

Jared: On land stolen from Native Americans.

Amir: Shouldn't we have to learn about all of them too?

Dr. Yeh: A grounding breath, please.

Everyone: [*Breathes.*]

Dr. Yeh: Excellent. This is a great discussion, but let's get back on topic. The initial question still stands: How could the Constitution be used to address book banning?

John Preston: As *I* said, it can't—

Jared: It *could* be argued that banning books in public schools, which are partially federally funded, violates the First Amendment.

John Preston: Bro, *how?*

Dionte: "Abridging the freedom of speech" is how I think it's worded.

John Preston: [*Shakes his head.*] No way. Nobody is being prevented from speaking freely. The fact that the books even exist is proof of that.

Dr. Yeh: A very interesting argument, Mr. LePlante. Anyone else?

Everyone: [*Silence.*]

Dr. Yeh: No one?

Dionte: I mean . . . I guess depending on *which* books are getting banned, it could be argued that the practice is discriminatory?

Dr. Yeh: Okay. Go on.

Dionte: Well, if there are clear commonalities between the books that are getting pulled, and said commonalities have to do with stuff like race or gender or religion or sexual orientation, one could make a case using the equal protection clause in the Fourteenth Amendment.

Amir: Right on, brutha!

John Preston: [*Shakes his head.*] Y'all are reaching. Equal protection only applies to living, breathing Americans. Whose rights are being violated here? A bunch of fictional characters? This argument is absurd.

Dionte: Books are written by living, breathing Americans, champ. We call them *authors*.

Everyone: [*Laughs.*]

John Preston: [*Looks like he's about to combust.*]

Imani: That's not to mention living, breathing American students. If only certain books are being taken away, the students in classrooms who are like the characters in the banned books could absolutely argue that they feel discriminated against. If I gotta read F. Scott Fitzgerald, you can read James Baldwin. Or better yet, somebody contemporary and, you know, alive.

Everyone: [. . .]

Ainsley: Well, I still don't think I should have to take an ethnic studies class.

Amir: You know that's a course *type*, right? Not an actual class. There are a lot of dope options . . . African American studies, Middle Eastern relations, history of Latin America—

Ainsley: Still irrelevant.

Imani: Aren't you half-Cuban?

Ainsley: What does *that* have to do with anything?

Everyone: [. . .]

John Preston: No offense, but what's the *point* of all this?

Amir: Mmm . . . you mean talking about the constitutionality of something in a constitutional law course?

John Preston: And this is precisely why I'm running for office. Students enroll here to learn things that are relevant to their futures as global leaders. This topic has nothing to do with the Constitution, so we shouldn't be discussing it in this course—

Dionte: Isn't caring, and therefore learning, about the different types of people you'll be representing the *most* relevant thing when you want to be a leader?

John Preston: Teachers need to follow the curriculum.

Jared: Bro, why do you even talk?

Dr. Yeh: A grounding breath, please.

Everyone: [*Breathes.*]

8

Ground of Public Confidence

Jared is speed-walking across campus that afternoon, late to a meeting with his campaign team, when he starts to feel like he's being side-eyed. He tries to brush it off as paranoia at first—he's admittedly still a bit shaken by the Constitutional Law conversation (it's not like he's never made the *How is this relevant to me?* argument before . . .)—but when he passes a small cadre of girls and hears "Oh my god, is that *him?*" he knows something's amiss.

He checks his fly. It's zipped. Looks down . . . shirt seems to be clean. Is there something on his face, maybe?

As he climbs the steps to the student center, four people glance at him and quickly look away. He pulls open a door and could swear he hears a guy say "Yeeks" as their paths cross.

Still, Jared tries to shake it off.

Walking up to the meeting room Amir reserved and seeing the

pandemonium inside, however? Zero question: Something has gone terribly wrong.

"Jared's here," comes a female voice from somewhere within the frenzy. There are a bunch of people gathered around the long table at the center of the room, shuffling papers and speaking in low but palpably terse voices, as well as two people on laptops in opposite corners and one person whispering angrily into a cell phone.

"Uhhh . . ."

Amir's head pops up at the head of the table. "Don't you worry, Jare-Bear!" he says with a salute before ducking down again. "We got it aaaaaaall under control."

"This is *slander,* Ms. Park," barks the person on the phone— Aaron Karo, Jared realizes. "There is zero evidence to support the accusation. And the Undergraduate College Council needs to make a statement. The reputation of your organization is on the line if a candidate for office can be openly subjected to this sort of public abuse— What do you *mean,* 'abuse' is hyperbolic?"

Jared's pulse quickens as he steps closer to the chaos. Whatever this is, it's bad. He can feel it.

Printouts are scattered all over the table. Jared reaches for one, and a hand wraps around his wrist. He looks up into the face of Pat Neuman. "Don't worry about it, okay, bro? We're nipping it in the bud."

Jared wants to ask Pat what the hot holy hell he's talking about, but he can't get his mouth to form words. It's like his brain has had to process too much over the past sixteen hours and is giving up the ghost. Pat lets go of Jared's arm, and Jared brings one of the sheets into his line of sight. It's . . . a flyer. It's got the same picture of him sitting below VOTE JARED PETER CHRISTENSEN FOR JUNIOR CLASS COUNCIL PRESIDENT! that his campaign flyers have, but said picture has been defaced: There are Xs over the eyes and a crudely drawn tongue hanging out of the mouth. Both of which were added digitally.

The worst part, however, is what's printed below his photo. Instead of the QR code that leads to his well-designed campaign page, there's an acronym:

S.A.C.C.C.T.D.D.

Students Against Class Council Candidates That Drive Drunk

And now Jared finds his words. "WHAT THE FU—"

His phone rings.

And keeps ringing. Because when he sees who's calling, he's too stunned to answer.

It stops.

And then starts ringing again.

Is she really calling him *now*? After *three days* of not responding to his texts?

It stops ringing again.

And restarts.

"Maybe answer it?" comes a voice from behind him. Robbie. Who hasn't looked up from his laptop. "Doesn't seem like they're going to give up."

It stops and starts again. Jared slides his thumb across the top of the screen and lifts the device to his ear. "Hello?"

"Jesus, don't *scare* me like that," Dylan says.

Which . . . is confusing? "What?"

"I dunno!" She really does sound panicked. Definitely not what Jared would've expected. "I thought you got pulled into a disciplinary meeting or something! Or maybe they came and arrested you?"

"Are you asking me or telling me?" It's the most absurd thing he could possibly say, considering the circumstances, but Jared has no idea what to make of what sounds like genuine concern flowing into his ears in a voice that is quite literally giving him goose bumps. Doesn't help that the last time he saw the face of the person speaking, he was looking at a pair of mug shots.

It is by far the most befuddling thing he's ever experienced.

"Wow, you are *clearly* in shock," Dylan says.

Jared doesn't reply. (She might be right? Seems probable . . .)

"Jared?" she continues. "Are you there?"

Amir looks up, and Jared points to his phone to indicate that he's going to take the call outside. "Yeah, I'm here," he finally responds, exiting the room.

"Okay. I'm pulling them down everywhere I see them, and I've got my team on it too."

More confusion. "Huh? Pulling what down?"

"Umm . . . the smear flyers? Have you not seen them?"

"Oh." *Why would she pull them down if she's behind them?* says a voice in Jared's head. "Yeah, I saw them."

"You sure you're okay?"

"Who said I'm okay?" The words surprise Jared. But the truth of them, and the sound of his own voice saying them, seems to pull him back into his skin. Which is covering his body. Which is here on campus . . . and which is now embroiled in something very unpleasant, if his churning gut is any indication.

"Look, I'm about a three-minute walk from your apartment," she says. "You want me to meet you there?"

Why? is what Jared wants to say. *Why would I meet you at my apartment? Who even* are *you? Why did you call me? Is this some sort of sick game?*

What comes out instead: "Yeah. I'd really appreciate that. I should be there in six."

Neither of them says a word outside the building. She just stands aside as he punches in the last four digits of his student number and his entry code, and then she falls in line behind him. He goes straight to his room once they're inside the apartment, and she stays right on his heels.

"Should I shut it?" she says, pointing to his bedroom door. It registers that the girl who has been on his mind nonstop for the past week is now standing in the most personal and intimate space he has outside of home. But Jared has precisely zero feelings about it. He's just . . . numb. She's rocking long braids that make her scalp look like a checkerboard—if this is a wig too, it's a really cool one—and, as usual, her skin seems to glow. But this time, as soon as their eyes meet, he gets a flash of her mug shot.

"Nah, leave it open," he says. "Actually . . . let's go to the living room."

They do. And they sit. And after what feels like an eons-long silence, she turns to him. "Is it okay if I touch you?" she asks.

Again: very unexpected. But (also again) Jared's mouth is saying "Of course" before he has time to think.

She puts one hand on his knee—super gently at first, but then with more pressure—and the other on his shoulder.

And just like that, the tension melts away. He's so relieved, his head drops back and his eyes close. "Are you a witch or something?" he says without thinking.

Silence.

He cracks an eye to look at her. And she bursts out laughing.

"No, seriously," Jared continues, letting his eyes close again. He couldn't censor himself right now if he tried, so . . . he doesn't. "It doesn't even make sense that you're *here*. Let alone turning my body to butterscotch pudding with the touch of your chocolate hands."

"Vanilla."

"What?" Jared says.

"Vanilla pudding. Your tan is decent, but definitely don't have enough melanin to be butterscotch. And don't describe Black people in food terms."

At this, Jared opens both eyes and turns to face her fully. "What are you doing here, Dylan?"

She drops her eyes and doesn't respond.

"Like, you rushed out of here *days* ago, haven't replied to *any* of my messages asking how you're doing, and now this thing only *you* know about me is all over campus a *day* after our campaigns launch? And you're suddenly Captain Save-a-Ho?"

That *only you know* bit isn't true, of course—Justyce and Amir know, but *they* certainly wouldn't launch a perfectly timed smear campaign—but the last thing Jared said seems to be the only thing Dylan heard.

"Captain *what,* now?" she asks.

"I learned it from that best friend who passed away. He said it's used to describe a person who only shows up when someone seemingly needs rescue."

She snorts. "I know what it means, Jared. Just surprised to hear you use it."

"My other questions stand, Dylan."

She clasps her hands in her lap and takes a deep breath. "Okay," she says. "All of that is reasonable. You want me to take it point by point?"

"That would be appreciated."

She nods. "Point one: I rushed out because my lawyer called—"

"Your *lawyer?*" It's not *that* surprising, knowing what he knows, but hearing her say it so openly catches him off guard.

"It's a long story, and I give you my word that I'll tell you about it someday, but I can't yet because I'm still in the thick of some things involving my old school."

Hmm. "Okay . . ."

"The messages thing . . . ugh." She puts her head in her hands. (Really full of surprises, this one.) "Look, this probably won't make sense to you at all, but I have this thing—it's rooted in an anxiety disorder I developed as a result of the other thing I can't talk about?"

"Are you asking me or telling me?" Jared says again, unable to resist.

"Really? Now?" But she smiles. Some of the tightness eases out of the room. "Long story short, if someone asks me if I'm okay and I'm not okay, I just . . . don't respond. Like I was perfectly fine *overall,* but I knew that you were asking in reference to something I'm actually *not* okay about, so . . . I got stuck. I'm really sorry."

Jared hopes she's not going to wait for him to respond because he has no *idea* what to say to that.

Thankfully, she continues. "And then the Captain Save-a-Ho bit, as you put it. First, please know that *I did not do this,* Jared. Not sure if that's what you were implying with the 'only *you* know' part of that inquisition, but this was *not* me. Throwing my partner on a project worth a quarter of my grade under the bus—and at a *new* school? Yeah, hard no."

Jared grunts. "Fair point."

"And I 'showed up' because it pissed me off seeing somebody trying to take you down. You're a good dude, Jared. Hate to admit it, but I kinda like you."

Jared's eyebrows rise. "Oh, really?"

"Don't let it go to your head," she says, smacking his arm. Flirtatiously. (Jared Peter Christensen is fully aware of when he's being flirted with.) "I primarily mean 'like you' as a *person*—"

"*Secondarily,* though?" And he makes those eyebrows wiggle.

"Oh my god, you're such a child," she says, rolling her eyes before looking him over. "I mean you're *all right,* I guess. Smart*ish.* *Sort of* attractive. *Decent* to be around in a place that isn't always comfortable for me. Or whatever . . ."

"You're hedging because I'm white, aren't you?"

The question hangs in the air for a second. And then they both explode into laughter. "I really can't stand you," she says, wiping tears from her face.

"Hey, Dylan?"

They lock eyes.

"You promise you didn't do this?"

She raises her right hand. "Swear it on my merit-based scholarships."

Jared takes a deep breath and nods. Even if he decides to believe her—and for now, he does—it doesn't bring him any comfort. No, the flyers don't contain any proof of anything, but clearly somebody he *can't* trust knows his secret.

Just like somebody *she* certainly can't trust knows hers.

Still, though: They both know those fliers were accurate and Jared shouldn't be in the race. Is she letting that part slide because she has a secret too?

His phone rings. Amir.

They exchange a look, and she nods in understanding. "I'll let myself out," she says, standing up. "You'll let me know if you need something?"

Jared's eyes narrow. "Not sure," he says. It's the most honest he's been in a while. Feels kinda good. "Respectfully."

She smiles. "You're something else," she says. "But I get it. We'll talk soon. Cuz you know: project."

He answers the phone as he watches her leave. "Hello?"

"Got it under control," Amir says in his ear. "We're back on track. Feel free to breathe."

Jared does.

And all he smells is Dylan Coleman.

9

Beneficent Ends

Turns out "under control" is an understatement. Not only did the UCC post a written statement denouncing the allegations against Junior Class Council presidential candidate Jared Christensen as "patently untrue"—in bold, at the top of the UCC election website, where it couldn't possibly be missed—but they also posted a video about how *slander tactics and libelous campaign rhetoric are a powerful and insidious threat to true democracy.*

Jared couldn't figure out exactly how to feel about it. He was relieved, obviously. Who wouldn't be? Could even say he felt a little vindicated: Someone attempted to take him out of the game and failed.

But Jared is also very much aware of the fact that . . . well, the "allegations" aren't actually false.

Though he tries not to think too much about it (because what would be the point?), it's this awareness that keeps him from responding when Dylan reaches out to check on him the following morning after the statement and video go live.

She seems sincere enough:

> Saw the statement. Thank GOD.

> I still can't believe someone actually did that! You okay?

After she left yesterday, he made sure his read receipts were off so he'd have time to process any messages she sent without her knowing he saw them. As odd as it feels to admit, he now understands why she didn't respond to *him* . . . but he still can't bring himself to write back. Because what would he even say? Is she really feeling *nothing* over the fact that he's getting away with something they both know shattered a Black guy's pro-football dreams?

Someone else he finds himself avoiding: Justyce. Because Justyce also knows the UCC response is based on a lie. So this morning he waits until he hears Justyce leaving the apartment before he opens his bedroom door. Does he feel like a coward? Absolutely. But Jared frankly doesn't have it in him to see his old friend, who has been both wrongfully arrested *and* shot by a police officer.

He pulls his baseball cap low and walks across campus with his head down and his hands tucked into the kangaroo pocket of his hoodie, hoping against hope that it'll prevent him from being recognized. Yesterday's experience wasn't tremendous, and though the UCC correction is out there, it's impossible to know who has seen it and, more importantly, who *believes* it.

He's vaguely relieved when he gets to the frat house, where he's due for a meeting, even though (1) he hates his fraternity and only rushed because his dad had been in it, and (2) he *knows* he'll be met with some stupidity inside. "Way to almost get kicked outta your presidential race, asshat," someone says as he walks in. Jared has no idea who because the guy pushes the bill of Jared's hat down in passing, thereby knocking his chin into his chest.

See?

Jared hangs a left into the hallway just before the grand staircase and heads toward the study.

"Christensen, you're late," comes a voice, from behind him this time. Jared checks his watch. He is, in fact, three minutes early. He peeks over his shoulder, ready to lob an insulting retort at the speaker . . . but then clamps his teeth together and swallows it back down. It's Hunter Landis, their chapter president. "Five minutes early is on time. Three is late."

"My sincerest apologies, Hunter."

The older boy falls in line beside Jared—who would love nothing more than to turn to vapor now. He has exactly zero love for the graduating senior, but the guy certainly commands respect. Reminds Jared of his dad (who also served as chapter president) . . . and he hates it with the fire of ultra-spicy food making its way into a toilet post-digestion. "I saw your little dustup. All's been rectified, I presume?"

"Yeah, everything's under control. UCC released a statement and video in my defense."

"Good to be one of *us,* isn't it?" Hunter elbows Jared and winks.

Jared gets hit with a wave of nausea. Largely because even

though he's not *exactly* sure what Hunter means by that, he can't dispute it. Makes him want to scream and punch the guy in the face.

He stays a little sick to his stomach as he enters the house conference room and the meeting begins. It's all about the fraternity's annual Spring Sting, the biggest (and most infamous) party they have all year. And despite being co-chair of the planning committee, Jared can only think about how at the last one, a brother had too much to drink and went on a tirade about how there were "too many goddamn Asians on campus." Someone took offense and called campus police, but when they showed up, instead of shutting the party down, the pair of cops took the bottles of top-shelf scotch they were offered and pretended they hadn't seen all the underage drinking.

Funny enough, the idiot who made the undeniably racist statement is yabbering on about being "more judicious when it comes to who we let in this year" when Dylan texts Jared again:

> I take it you now understand why I didn't text you back? 😅

> Let me know you're alive once you feel up to it.

That almost makes him smile, but then he hears someone mention the party date and realizes it's the same night as his JCC presidential debate. Which means he'll arrive late to the party that it's his job to plan because he'll be publicly opposing the political perspectives held by most of his fraternity brothers.

Seriously, universe?

He cuts his eyes at Hunter—who will surely ream Jared out about it just because he can. Best thing Jared can do right now is pour everything he's got into his planning duties so *this* year's party will be the best one yet. (The irony isn't lost on him.)

And it works. Literal hours go by with him immersed in catering and decorating research. And when his phone rings four and a half of them later, he feels like he's being jolted out of a dream.

It's Dylan.

He stares at the phone in shock for so long, it stops ringing. (It occurs to him that this happens every time she calls.)

But then it starts again.

"Hey, Dylan," he says, picking up. "Sorry I missed—"

"Jared? Thank god," comes her panicked voice into his ear buds. "Apologies for cold-calling you like this, but I have a situation over here and could really use your help."

He's out of his seat and shoving his laptop into his bag before he can register the movement. "What's wrong? You okay?" In the hallway and headed to the front door.

"There's this *girl.* I just . . . Can you come, please?" she says. "I'm in the common room at Bradford."

The second Jared's feet hit the pavement outside, he takes off at a run. "I'll be right there."

By the time Jared arrives five minutes later, the common room Dylan mentioned is a battlefield. Dylan is sitting in a chair with her head in her hands as a red-faced white girl—grungy sweatshirt, Hello Kitty pajama pants, messy blond bun on top of her head, dirty Ugg boots—shouts at her from across the room. There are two campus police officers standing to the side doing absolutely nothing, and a room full of disgruntled students Jared is sure were told not to leave (the supposed "standard protocol" when campus police get involved).

"I know you took it!" the white girl is yelling. There's another girl beside her, seemingly holding her back. "Just return it so everyone can leave!"

Jared rushes over and kneels in front of Dylan. "Hey, I'm here," he says, gently putting a hand on her knee. "What's going on?"

When she lifts her face and Jared sees that she's crying, a geyser of rage shoots up from his midsection through his chest and throat and right into his brain, burning every shred of rationality. He doesn't know who did what, but tears on Dylan's face have him ready to set the whole campus ablaze . . . maybe even the entire state of Connecticut.

"That girl swears I stole her laptop," Dylan says. "Claims she went to the bathroom as her friends were leaving, and when she came back it was gone."

Jared looks over his shoulder at the other girl. She's glaring at him now.

Good.

"She consider that maybe one of her 'friends' took it?" he says, still staring her down and loud enough for her to hear him. Then he turns back to Dylan so *no one* has any question about where his loyalties lie.

"Oh, I definitely suggested that," Dylan replies. "But she wouldn't hear a word of it. Called me a 'Black bitch' and then immediately called these idiot cops—"

"Young man, you can't be here." One of the police officers

has appeared above Jared's right shoulder. "This is an active crime scene."

That does it.

"Excuse me?" Jared says, standing up. He's taller than the policeman, and it's clear by the way the officer takes a step backward that he wasn't expecting Jared's height. "Where is the evidence of a crime, *officer*?"

"That young lady says this one stole her computer—"

"And *this* young lady says she did no such thing. Did you have *that* young lady call the friends who were with her to see if one of them grabbed it by mistake? Or consult any witnesses?"

"You trying to tell me how to do my job, son?"

"I'm not your *son*," Jared says, blood boiling. "And if anything, what I'm trying to do is help you *keep* your job. You know how bad it looks for you to hold all these people here off an accusation a white girl is making against a Black student with zero evidence?"

The officer pales. "Exactly what are you insinuating?"

A throat clears on the other side of the room. "Did anyone *see* this young lady take the other one's laptop?" the other officer asks.

"No," a guy says from a corner. "Can we go now?"

"I'm sorry, that won't be possible until this matter is resolved."

Everyone groans, and collective cursing ensues.

"This is bullshit—"

"Dude, we're not even *involved*—"

"It seriously *cannot* be legal for them to hold us here—"

"I'm calling my grandfather. He's on the board—"

A phone rings, chopping through the tension. The accuser's. She picks up. "Hello?"

The room goes quiet.

"Yeah, I'm still here," she continues. "This *girl* took my laptop and won't give— What? Really?" Her face goes ghost white. "You're sure?" She glances around the room. "Okay. I'm coming."

She hangs up. The silence in the room is so loud, it might as well be thunder. "Never mind," the girl says, beginning to gather her things.

"Oh, no way," Jared says. "Nope." He walks over to her, phone in hand. When she turns to him, he snaps a picture of her face.

"You better delete that!" She grabs for the phone, but he stretches it out of her reach.

"Anyone know this young lady's name?" Jared asks the room.

"Morgan Delaine," comes a voice. (*Gotta love a good snitch,* Jared thinks.)

"And what year are you, Morgan?" he says to the girl.

"Like I would tell you. Can you move?"

Jared doesn't budge.

"Officers, can you not see that this guy is *threatening* me?" she says, edging into hysteria. "Aren't you going to do something about it?"

Jared laughs. "Sweetheart, there's a room full of people here who can attest to the fact that you're not being threatened in any way. I am, however, *promising* you that I'm making it my mission to ensure that you face consequences for the racist accusation and insult you threw at my friend here. Anything you want to say to this girl, Dylan?"

"Nope," comes Dylan's reply. "Can we go now?" She looks the officer who confronted Jared right in the eye.

"We presume your laptop's been found, miss?" the other officer says.

The girl—Morgan—crosses her arms and refuses to reply. The move is so John Preston LePlante IV, Jared wants to scream.

"Jesus, can you just say yes?" comes the voice of another student in the room. "We'd *all* like to leave now."

She scowls for a few beats longer, then her eyes fill with tears. "Fine. Yes."

"Yes, it's been found?" the other officer says.

"I said yes!" She drops down in a chair and starts sobbing into her hands.

"Fantastic," Dylan says, standing and grabbing her bag. She heads straight for the exit. "Let's go, Jared."

April 13

Dear Munny,

First, let's just get the bombshell out of the way: Dylan slept over.

"HUH?" you might be thinking. "How did you get to that point so quickly?"

Well, it's far more devastating than exciting. Which is why I'm writing to you yet again.

Last night, I bore witness to the kind of racism you and Justyce were trying to get me to acknowledge two and a half years ago. I won't go into detail about the incident itself, but the second Dylan and I made it back to my apartment and the door closed behind us, she like . . . dissolved. Just fell against me, weeping like I'd never seen anyone weep before. I tried to lead her to the couch, but she asked to go to my room instead. "In case your roommate is here or comes in. I don't want anybody else seeing me like this."

Next thing I knew, we were stretched out on my bed with me holding her while she soaked my shirt with her tears. And like . . . I started crying too, Manny! I felt so helpless to do anything about how upset she was, and the whole situation was so messed up, and I had so much <u>anger</u> inside, it all just built up and decided to spill out of my eyeballs.

The last time I cried was after getting that DUI, but the time before that was when I heard you died. I did my best to keep it together so she wouldn't know, but I had one of those super-strong sniffle inhales, and it shook my chest. So she looked up.

"Oh my god, are you crying too? Jared!" And she climbed out of the bed and made her way to my bathroom. Definitely panicked—it's nowhere near as clean as Justyce's—but she came back with a box of tissues.

"Wow, _I_ should've gotten these for _you_," I said, shifting to sit on the edge of the bed. "I am clearly a trash consoler. Please forgive me."

It made her laugh. "I mean, I was kind of ON you, so we'll just say you couldn't move" was her reply. "Also, if you think I could _possibly_ be mad at you after everything you just did . . ." She shook her head. "AND you're crying with me?"

Then she gave me this _look_. Like, yes: The Ex used to goo-goo eye me all the time, but MAN, does it feel different when you actually _like_ the girl who's looking at you like you're personally responsible for all the light in the world. I legit thought my chest was gonna explode.

"Dylan, are you okay?" I asked then. A stupid question, for sure, considering the circumstances, but it was all I had at the moment.

"I am now," she said. And she sat down beside me and put her head on my shoulder. Dude, I don't even have words for the things I felt right then. I just know it's a moment I'll remember forever.

Anyway, she eyeballed my face again, and then her gaze dropped to my lips. And as much as I wanted to lean into that shit and kiss her with everything I had—and I had a LOT at that moment, let me tell you—I couldn't do it. No idea when the hell I got so noble, but the fact that I knew she'd just been through something awful and was super vulnerable made me press the pause button.

Which turned out to be the right choice. I told her that if she wanted to talk about what she was feeling, I would listen without comment. And at first, she just shut down.

But then I told her about how I felt when I first heard that you and Justyce were shot, and you didn't make it. "Dylan, I know I'll never experience the other side of this or understand how it feels to be in your shoes, but if you need someone to share the load with, I'll gladly take on as much as I can for you."

She started crying again.

The whole thing is so messed up, Manny. Like she started telling me about how stuck she felt—the moment that stupid girl accused her of theft, Dylan knew she couldn't walk out without things escalating. She also knew she couldn't do a thing when the girl "called me out the name my mama gave me" as she put it. "The moment I popped off on her would've been the moment I became the villain, despite not having done anything wrong." And then when campus police showed up, she said her life legit flashed before her eyes. "These situations can go so wrong so fast," she said.

She was right. What happened to you and Jus is proof of it.

The wildest part, Manny? When this girl realized she was wrong about Dylan, she didn't even apologize! She was just gonna up and leave with ZERO admission of wrongdoing, and the cops 100% would've let her! You remember that football player I told you about? D'Squared? Despite being EXPELLED, he still issued a public apology. You know, because higher-ups can't have the Black guy making the team or our school "look bad."

All I could think about during the incident—you know, other than hulking out and smashing everything in sight—was how absurd it was that this white girl could literally call campus police (!!!) with ZERO EVIDENCE to support her claim, and Dylan had to sit there and take it. This might sound random, but the equal protection clause from the Fourteenth Amendment came up in Constitutional Law yesterday, and I really feel like I get why it's so important now. Literally no one came to Dylan's defense, Manny. Room FULL of other students, none of whom saw her take the computer, and no one said a word to support her.

It was so messed up, dude.

Back to the sleepover bit: So she gets done telling me how she feels, and then she turns so she's facing me. "Can we kiss?" she said.

"Uhhh . . ." (Not my smoothest response, but cut me some slack, all right? I'd just resisted doing the exact thing she was asking for, I THOUGHT for good reason.)

"I'd really like to kiss you, Jared," she went on. "And not just because you played Captain Save-a-Ho."

I'd called her that just yesterday (though it feels like an eon ago) so I had to laugh at that one.

"I'm serious," she said. "Not that I'm a ho, but you get what I mean. I'm still not sure what it is about you, but I like you, Jared. This was a shitty night, and it'd be lovely to end it on a different note." She leaned closer. "So, may I kiss you?"

No clue what _I_ said, but it must've been something affirmative because we started kissing. And bro, her lips are the juiciest, fluffiest, pillowiest lips I've ever had the pleasure of putting my far-less-amazing lips on. She seemed to enjoy it, though, because when we broke apart (some time later, I might add), she was smiling.

Then she asked if she could stay with me.

"I don't want to have sex or anything, but I feel very safe here with you, and I kinda need that right now." (Very straightforward, this girl.)

So I gave her some sweats and one of my T-shirts, ordered us some Thai food, and she introduced me to Spike Lee's _Do the Right Thing_ (legit need a whole other letter to unpack _that_ one). Then we curled up together and went to sleep.

She was gone when I woke up this morning, but she left a note (my true reason I'm writing to you). I've taped it here in this notebook for you to read.

Dear Jared,

First, thank you again for last night. You're very sweet, and falling asleep beside you was lovely. You whistle when you're in REM, by the way. It's cute.

Anyway, I want to confess something: As much as I appreciate all you did for me, once the adrenaline was gone and I woke up in your arms, I had some anger inside me about it. There I was, having done nothing wrong, and you just swooped in, talked to those cops hella sideways, and got exactly the result you wanted.

It was a sore but necessary reminder for me of why I decided to run for JCC president. As much as other Black students need to see someone who looks like them in an elected college council position, white students—students of ALL ethnic backgrounds, in fact—really need to see it too. If there's one thing I've learned from Dr. Yeh's class, it's that sometimes you have to get in there and _make_ the changes that align with equity and justice, knowing people will eventually adjust, instead of trying to get everyone on board beforehand.

In other words, I'm so thankful you came to rescue me, but I also hate that you had to. Perhaps if girls like Morgan encountered people like me in positions that convey respect and authority, she wouldn't have fixed her lipless mouth (sorry, still mad) to say and do what she did.

That said, please forgive me for vanishing while you were sleeping. Feel free to call or text me when you wake up.

—Dyl

After seeing what I saw, hearing her heart, and then reading that note . . . Bro, I can't believe I'm writing this, but she really might be the better candidate for JCC president.

The thing is: Even KNOWING that, I still want to win. It felt GOOD to put that Morgan girl in her place. Let her know that her actions wouldn't go unpunished, and she doesn't get to pretend it never happened. It felt RIGHT. JUST, even.

So why am I so uncomfortable?

Maybe I am feeling a way about how she just vanished again. Though I did get an explanation this time . . .

I'm gonna try to go back to sleep.

More soon, I guess.

—Jared

April 13

Dear Manny,

Yeah, I know it's only been a few hours since my last letter, but PLOT TWIST:

    My parents are coming to visit. Tomorrow.

    Again: If you're with God or whatever, let him know I could REALLY use a break from all this "testing" or whatever. Thanks.

—Jared

10

Redress of Grievances

Jared prepares for his parents' visit the best that he can. He really does. Cleans his room and bathroom top to bottom (even though washing the scent of Dylan from his sheets and pillowcase feels like murdering a dream). He gets a haircut and trims his nails and irons his slacks and shirt. He checks his grades and wipes the screens of his laptop, phone, and tablet. He makes sure he's ready to answer any questions the parents might have about his life at school.

And he really does *feel* ready. He takes some of Dr. Yeh's grounding breaths on the way to the restaurant in the car they sent for him (which is ridiculous, but he even does a decent job of not thinking too much about it). And by the time he's standing in front of the restaurant, Jared is moderately calm. In fact, when it occurs to him that he hasn't seen his folks since spring break, he realizes he kind of misses them. Maybe they miss him too and that's why they came to visit. . . .

He strides in, chin high. Gives the host his name, is met with an "Ah, yes, your family is waiting for you"—a red flag, though he misses it—and is led through the main dining room to a more private space at the back.

"There he is, the rascal!" comes a voice Jared is *not* expecting to hear.

And with that, he knows the evening is shot to hell.

"Get over here, you little punk." Jared is yanked into a headlock and given a very painful knuckled rub at the center of his scalp.

There goes his perfect hair.

He tries with all his might to just take the assault without making a sound, but that makes the nitwit torturing him squeeze his neck tighter and knuckle in deeper.

Jared is suddenly eleven again. "Oww, Justin! Get off!"

"Ah, you kids!" comes Dad's voice. Jared knows the old man is enjoying every minute of watching his older, spitting-image son whale on the younger, weaker one he'd prefer not to claim. Even if the brutality is happening in a two-Michelin-star restaurant.

"Can you tell him to get off me, please?" Jared pleads.

"That's enough, Justin," their mother says.

Justin lets go and shoves Jared with far more force than could ever be warranted.

"What is *he* doing here?" Jared asks as he takes the seat across from his moron brother. Thankfully the table is big and round, and Jared is out of kicking range. Justin Paul Christensen is eight years Jared's senior and happily married to the girl their dad set him up with when *he* was an undergrad—though he went to a different Ivy on a full (and wholly unnecessary) national merit scholarship. Despite all that *and* his wildly successful investment banking career, Justin would never pass up an opportunity to cause bodily harm to his baby bro.

Jared despises him.

"Your brother had a big acquisition meeting a couple towns over—" Dad begins.

"And, of course, closed the deal," Justin says, bowing.

"Attaboy!" from Dad. Loudly.

"How are you, sweetheart?" Mom.

Good ol' Mom. Always remembers Jared exists. Makes him sit up a little taller. "I'm doing all right, Mom. Thank you for asking."

"Grades are good," from Dad. (He's telling Jared, not asking.)

"I have one class this semester that's a bit of a challenge, but currently sitting at a high A-minus and holding a three-point-nine-seven overall."

Dad nods. No smile. No *Good job, son!* "Which class is the trouble?"

"Constitutional Law."

Dad snorts and looks away. Waves to get the attention of the server.

"The hell you taking that crap for?" Justin asks, leaning back in his seat and crossing his arms.

"Oh, you don't know?" Dad says, sarcasm dripping. "Our little Jared decided he wants to be a civil rights attorney. He's also running for class president and has some sort of *woke* agenda."

Which . . . how could Dad possibly know that? Jared certainly didn't tell him or Mom (who he knew would tell Dad). He planned to tell them both eventually. Was just hoping to win first.

"His fraternity president told me all about it during a call last week about how our most recent donation is being allocated," Dad continues, the look on his face reading *Just when I thought I couldn't be more disappointed . . .*

Justin barks a laugh. "Are you an idiot? Where's the money in civil rights law?"

"Not everything's about money, you know," Jared says, mostly under his breath. He feels even more like a little kid than when he was being noogied. He'd really like to get up and walk out.

"Oh god, don't tell me you're on some socialist garbage," Justin says.

The server has appeared at the table. "I'd like a Macallan neat, the lady here will have a six-ounce pour of your best pinot gris, and the young one there will have a Perrier. Justin? Beverage?"

"I don't really want a Perrier," Jared pipes up. Feels good to defy Dad so openly. "I'll take a ginger ale, please."

"Give me a Woodford," from Justin. Who doesn't even look at the server. Jared's big bro's vibe is very John Preston LePlante IV, and Jared can't stand it. He also can't stand that his rival keeps popping into his head unbidden. "Now what's this *law* thing about?" Justin continues to Jared.

"No offense, but it's really none of your business, Justin," Jared replies.

Dad and Justin lock eyes then, and everything becomes clear:

Justin was invited to dinner to back Dad up. Be an additional voice of dissent regarding Jared's "life choices."

Jared should've known.

The server comes back with the drinks and takes everyone's dinner orders, and for the most part, Dad and his *preferred* son get so wrapped up in finance talk, Jared's able to remain a nonentity. Occasionally, Mom reaches out and pats his hand. And though his self-esteem takes a beating—the number of passive-aggressive jabs aimed at him is staggering—he's relieved to get through the meal without having to say much.

When the check comes, Justin takes it, and Jared turns away to roll his eyes under the guise of cracking his back. It's almost over, this farce of a "family dinner." Just a couple more minutes in the car with the parents, and he can go back to his very separate, very different life.

But then the valet pulls Justin's grotesquely conspicuous bright blue electric Porsche around, and Dad tells him to drop Mom off at their hotel. "I'll be there soon," Dad says to her. "I'd like to spend some more time with our son. Maybe take a stroll down memory lane while I'm at it, you know? Told the Landis kid I'd even swing by the fraternity house."

Thus, a new round of horrors begins.

Dad gets a call as soon as they're in the car he ordered for them, and he stays on the phone for the duration of the drive back to campus. (Perhaps Manny *did* put in a good word for Jared with the divine entity upstairs.) Dad has them dropped at the residential college where *he* lived for all four years, and through the eight-minute walk between there and the frat house, the old man reminisces on his experience as a "working class, first-generation college kid on financial aid whose only option was success."

As Bill Christensen, a man Jared has only ever known to be hyper-confident about his place in the world, talks about feeling out of place around the wealthy kids he went to this school with, it occurs to Jared how ironic it is that his dad has so much disdain for things like equity and inclusion.

Why wouldn't he want his son to help students like the one *he* was? Because they're a different race than him?

But a different man walks into the frat house and greets Hunter Landis as though Hunter is his *real* son and Jared's just some stray puppy he can't shake loose. Watching the two of them embrace hits Jared like a blow to the sternum, and tears spring to his eyes. He trails them through the house, vaguely listening as Dad asks how certain traditions are being upheld and what *great legacy* Hunter would like to leave behind as chapter president.

"What about you, Jared?" Hunter asks, snatching Jared fully back to reality.

"Huh?"

Hunter smiles, thrilled at having caught Jared off guard in front of his father. "Junior Class Council president is cool or whatever, but you surely intend to follow in your dad's footsteps and become president of *this* organization, yeah? It's in your blood, man." He shoves Jared's shoulder.

"Oh, yeah," Jared says. "Of course."

Why he's lying, he can't really say: He despises his fraternity and would like nothing more than to be free from it. But . . . well, he can't *say* that, can he? Not with the man who has paid for Jared's charmed existence watching his every move.

Dad *hmphs* and crosses his arms. "He'll definitely have to re-examine some of his guiding principles if he wants to lead an organization as rich and storied as—" His phone rings. (Jared sends another silent *thank you* up to the heavens.) "Yeah, honey? I'm still at the fraternity— All right. I'll head there."

"The wife has requested my return," Dad says to Hunter as he ends the call. "I'm gonna walk this guy to his apartment and then head out. Thanks for showing me around. Letting me relive the glory days for a spell."

"No problem at all, Mr. Christensen." They head toward the front door. "Perhaps you can convince your son to, you know, *engage* here a bit more frequently." He winks.

And then they're outside. And descending the porch steps. And moving away from the house.

So close to freedom, Jared can't even bring himself to be bothered by the jab Hunter threw at him as they left.

"We haven't talked about this campaign of yours," Dad says as they approach the student center. "Hunter sent me some screenshots of the platform you're running on."

Of course he did, the narc. "Is there something specific you'd like to know about it?" Jared asks, attempting to enter the conversation diplomatically.

"Well, I—"

But then someone calls Jared's name. And before he can even

register that it's happening, his head and body are rotating toward the sound. It's the voice he heard before falling asleep last night.

"Oh my god, hey!" Dylan says, bounding over and wrapping him in a hug. "Sorry I haven't gotten to reach out today—"

"And who might this be?" Dad asks. (Jared genuinely forgot the man was there for a second.)

"Oh man, my bad. Dylan, this is my dad, Bill Christensen. Dad, this is—"

"Dylan Marie Coleman." Dylan sticks her hand out for Dad to shake, but he's too busy looking back and forth between her and Jared to notice. Dylan takes the hint and drops her arm. "Pleasure to make your acquaintance?"

Dad gives Dylan a disapproving once-over that makes Jared cringe. He wants to say something but can't get his lips to move. "So, you're the one who wants to make 'ethnic studies' mandatory," Dad says.

Something flashes in Dylan's eyes, but she smiles. "Well, as the global majority is ethnically and culturally diverse, prioritizing learning about diverse people groups will increase students' chances of success during an era of increased globalization."

Dad literally snorts. Then turns to Jared. "When's the last time you spoke to Ainsley, son?"

"Huh?" Jared replies.

Dad's cheeks go pink. "Ainsley Cruz? You know, your girlfriend?"

"Ainsley's *not* my girlfriend, Dad." Jared's pulse races. He can't bring himself to look directly at Dylan. "I told you that—"

"Yeah, well . . ." And now Dad *does* look directly at Dylan.

With more contempt on his face than Jared's ever seen. "She should be."

"I'll catch you later, Jared," Dylan says, and she walks off.

Dad begins to walk in the opposite direction.

Jared looks back and forth between them . . .

Back . . . forth . . .

Forth . . . back . . .

And with a sigh, he follows his dad down the hill.

11

Assistance of Counsel

If Jared thought he felt bad about what happened with Dylan, SJ Friedman's expression when he tells her the story the following evening makes it way worse. "Can you maybe *not* look at me like I murdered a kitten in cold blood?" he says.

"And here I thought you were becoming a decent human being." SJ shakes her head. "Should've known better."

"Harsh, babe," from Justyce. Though he doesn't look up from his laptop screen.

Justyce, SJ, and Jared are sitting at a café inside the journalism school on SJ's university campus (which is a little over an hour drive from theirs). Jared enlisted their help in getting him ready for his upcoming presidential debate—having nationally ranked collegiate debate champions for friends has its perks.

Problem is, Jared was so distracted, SJ paused their failing preparations to investigate.

"Okay, let me make sure I understand correctly." SJ puts her pencil down. "Your dad looked her over like she was dog shit on the bottom of a shoe, openly disparaged her *excellent* argument for an ethnic studies course requirement, invoked your ex to her face, and you . . . just stood there?"

Jared puts his head in his hands. "I *froze,* okay? I didn't know what to do!"

SJ takes a deep breath and rubs her temples. "*Empathy,* Sarah-Jane," she says under her breath.

"Mm-hmm," from still-computer-focused Justyce.

"Okay," SJ begins. "I can understand the challenge of your position in that moment."

Well, this *is different . . . ,* Jared thinks but doesn't say.

SJ goes on. "But did you reach out and *tell her* any of that once you got back to your room? Please tell me you at least did *that,* Jared. . . ."

Jared's silence is so deafening, Justyce, who typically remains mum on Jared's love life, *does* look up from his laptop this time. "Come on, dawg! Are you *serious* right now?"

"It's not like she would've answered!"

"Bro, you still could've *tried.* Like, damn!"

"Also, I can almost guarantee she *would* have answered," SJ says. A salt-in-the-wound specialist, that one. "Honestly, if you'd reached out within a short-enough window and apologized profusely, she might've even been understanding. You're totally screwed now, though."

"Wow. Thank you, Sarah-Jane, for that resounding vote of confidence."

SJ shrugs. "No point in getting snarky with *me*. I'm just telling you the truth."

"Maybe all's not lost, dawg," Justyce says. "Y'all still have that project to complete, *and* you gotta see her at a bunch of election stuff, right? Plenty of opportunities to grovel your way back into her good graces—"

"*If* that's what you actually want," SJ cuts in, eyes narrowed. "Is it?"

And there it is, reason number 342 Jared Christensen has a love/hate relationship with SJ Friedman: It's like she can see the parts of his soul he tries to keep hidden—even from himself. Because though the answer is mostly *Yes, Jared would definitely like to get back in Dylan's good graces,* it's also . . . a little more complicated than that.

Frankly, Dylan deciding to never speak to him again would make his life less complicated. There was the project to complete, yes . . . But so long as they did their respective parts, additional communication wasn't *really* necessary, was it?

Maybe this was for the best. There was still a *lot* he didn't know about her, and this way, he didn't need to concern himself with stuff like her criminal history. He wouldn't have to stay on his toes or worry about being disowned by his father. (Jared couldn't put it past Bill Christensen to stop paying his tuition and write him out of the will for dating someone Dad didn't approve of.) There would be no more conflict over "caught-and-fraught feelings for a political rival," as Justyce put it. Jared could completely shift his focus to winning the election without experiencing any guilt over it.

However: Dylan still knew something about Jared that could threaten his victory. If she came forward now with what he told her, it would *really* cause problems. And not only for him: The whole Undergraduate College Council could be called to task for denying the allegations against him without doing the work of making sure they were false. Which was very easy to spin into either a race thing—especially when D'Squared's fate was taken into consideration—or some sort of accusation of preferential treatment for legacy students. Neither of which would be great.

"What's going on over there, J?" Justyce says, cutting into Jared's downward thought spiral.

He shakes his head clear. "Nothing. Let's get back into this debate prep."

SJ rolls her eyes. "Yes, of course. Let's flee our feelings. Which political issue would you like to hit first, Mr. Nothing?"

Jared stares at her blankly.

She turns and looks at Justyce. "This is really what you brought me to work with, Jus?"

Justyce shrugs. "Guess we gotta go ground up."

There's a huff from SJ. "Have you ever watched a political debate?" she asks Jared.

"Negative."

"My word, you are hopeless. Do you know what they're for, at least?"

"Uhh . . ." Jared glances at Justyce, starting to feel a smidge ashamed of how little he knows about Justyce's favorite pastime: Jus has been on their college debate team since the summer *before* their freshman year. "To hash out the most important issues of an election cycle?"

"In a literal sense, yes. But at the core, the aim is to make yourself look like the best person for the job out of the available options."

"Which goes beyond what you say," Justyce chimes in. "Yes, that part matters: It needs to be logical, evidence-based, and articulated in a way that's concise and easy to understand. But it also matters how you make people *feel*."

"Looking at the campaigns that are posted," SJ says, "you and Dylan have some similarities in your platforms. So *she's* your biggest concern in this debate. No matter how much work we do around honing your rhetoric and injecting emotional resonance into your responses, you'll have to stay on your toes to make sure that what you say either differs from or improves on what *she* says."

This makes Jared's heart rate spike. He's been so busy thinking about how to own John Preston in this thing, it didn't occur to him that the biggest threat to his victory would be the person who shares some of his perspectives. "But what about LePlante?"

"His perspectives are so wildly different from yours, you don't have to worry about standing out against him," SJ replies.

Jared looks at the screen of his open laptop and lets his eyes scan his opponents' campaign pages. John Preston's plans include dissolving *all* required courses, uprooting and penalizing any remaining affirmative action–based policies or practices in the admissions process, disbanding and outlawing all race- and ethnicity-based affinity groups on campus, and expanding the campus police force so that "their presence will be a palpable deterrent to criminal activity."

Interestingly, in combing through Dylan's platform, there

are *some* points that align with things Jared wants to see implemented: They both want to form recruitment teams to bring in more applicants from underrepresented demographics, and they both want to implement school-wide recognition of additional religious holidays, like Eid al-Adha, Yom Kippur, and Diwali. But some points in Dylan's campaign feel just as *intense* as some of John Preston's. Like she wants to form a committee that would "oversee all fraternity and sorority social events" to ensure that "no racist acts or themes are being committed or upheld." Jared understood the intention, but it felt like a slippery slope.

"We better be careful," SJ says, interrupting Jared's ponderings. "It looks like he's *thinking*. We know how dangerous that can be."

Justyce snorts.

"Really, Jus?" Jared says.

"Sorry, dawg. You gotta admit that was perfectly timed."

Jared sighs. "All of this feels . . . precarious," he says. "Like, reading through these other campaigns, I definitely get what you mean with regard to John Preston's ideas being at the opposite end of the spectrum from mine, but . . ." He stops.

"But what, man?" from Justyce.

Should he say it? He needs to, right? His friends are here to help him.

He takes a deep breath. "Well, some of Dylan's plans also seem a *tad* extreme. To me."

Justyce's eyebrows rise. Which makes Jared want to suck all the words back down and empty them into a toilet from his other end.

"We're listening," Justyce says.

"I mean, take the thing where she wants to demand 'full transparency' from the university when it comes to donation and admissions data. It's kind of a violation of privacy—"

"Mmmm . . . but is it?" SJ says. "Sounds to me like an attempt to keep people from buying their way in."

Definitely not gonna win that one. Jared moves on. "Okay. How about her proposed policy that would require quarterly DEI training for all faculty? Feels a *bit* over the top, doesn't it?" He holds his breath.

Justyce's face scrunches up in thought. "*Requiring* it is a bit aggressive, I'll agree. Though I do get the *spirit* behind the idea. Do you?"

"Of course I do," Jared replies.

"So *that's* what you need to lean into."

Which is when it clicks for Jared: Out of the three candidates in the race, he's the most moderate. The most *sensible*, even. All of his aims involve taking viable steps to diversify the student body and increasing support and visibility for organizations that serve students who aren't rich, straight, and white.

But . . . *is* that enough? Should he, like Dylan, be calling for greater transparency around admissions? Better yet: *Could* he? Yeah, he'd had the credentials to get in on merit, but he'd be lying if he pretended not to know about the sizable donation his dad's company made to the school when he got deferred.

These things were far more complicated than anyone wanted to admit. Was "fairness" even plausible in a system as old and convoluted as the one they were operating within?

SJ speaks again: "Okay, how 'bout we start by coming up with responses to things your opponents are addressing that you aren't."

"Like what?"

"Like legacy admissions," Justyce says pointedly. "And . . . DEI programming."

Two things he deliberately left out.

He lets his head drop onto the table with a thunk, and the moment his eyes are closed, he sees Dylan's face in his mind.

Who is he kidding? Of course he wants to get back in her good graces.

But first, he's gotta win an election.

April 16

Dear Manny,

Now, before I jump in here, I need to warn you that I am as mad as I was when we got into that little scuffle (aka, you kicked my ass) at basketball practice senior year.

What two-hand shoved me into the flames of rage this time? After an infuriating discussion in Constitutional Law—about a Black male teacher who was fired by his Black principal for teaching a book about a Black kid to a group of mostly Black students DURING BLACK HISTORY MONTH because one of two white students in the class complained to his parents ("Well, if he just stuck to the curriculum, this wouldn't have happened," John Preston asserted right before I laid into him and left)—I was walking across campus to my apartment when I spotted Dylan, talking and laughing with a group of other Black students. To catch you up, there was a bit of an incident involving my dad, and after discussing it with Justyce and SJ while working on my debate strategy a couple nights ago, I reached out a few times and even sent an apology voice note. Which she kept.

So I called her name and jogged over.

And like fine: I can admit that she didn't exactly look HAPPY to see me . . . she had her arms crossed and wasn't smiling. But I wasn't expecting her to be as rude as she was. Like, I asked her if she'd gotten my messages, and all she said was "Yep." No mention of how she felt about them or if she accepted my apology. And I get that she doesn't OWE me any of that . . . But this is the same girl who called ME for help and slept in MY bed four days ago.

I did my best to swallow my pride, you know? It had gotten quiet around us, but I tried to ignore it. "So you ready for the debate tomorrow?" I asked.

"At least as ready as you are," she replied.

Looking back, that was my cue to cut my losses and jet. But I couldn't, Manny. I just wanted her to talk to me. So I switched tactics: "Can we get a meetup on the books to knock this Yeh project out?"

"You sure you don't need your dad's approval first?"

I know my face went scarlet, but I held it together. It was a low blow for sure, but not completely unfair. Had it just been the two of us standing there, I might've said that aloud.

However, it wasn't just the two of us standing there, Manny. A fact that I was reminded of when one of her guy friends said, "Well, damn!"

That started what felt like an avalanche of insults. Another guy said, "It's that bad?" which was followed by "Wait, what the hell year is it?" and "Better question: How the hell old are we?"

What really took the cake was the last girl to speak. Her words: "Girl, I told you not to fool with these rich white boys."

Like what the hell, man? I don't even KNOW these people, and they're commenting on my life and saying things about me with ZERO information to go on? Dylan, of course, just stood there with a blank expression. I guess giving me a taste of my own medicine? (Seems beneath her, but who am I to judge?)

I managed to eke out a "Let me know when you're free so we can finish this thing" before I turned and walked away. But seriously, how dare they say stuff like that RIGHT in front of me? I'd stormed out of class earlier after defending the actions of a Black man to some bigoted idiot, and then these people I've never even SEEN before treat me like I'm some pampered Daddy's boy who can't make his own decisions?! And *if they knew the hell I go through trying to stand up for THEM—with full knowledge that it's causing me to lose my dad's respect—would they even care?*

I'm not "looking for a cookie," as SJ would say, but bro, NONE of this is easy. Yes, I have advantages I didn't earn, and yes, my starting line was different. But I'm still a human being just like they all are. One who is doing his best to make some positive changes for people who DON'T have my advantages and DIDN'T have my starting line, aka people like them. Is it too much to ask to be treated like a person?

I'm gonna go for a run. Thanks for listening.

Sincerely,
Jared

12

Speedy and Public Trial

When he looks back on it later, Jared will realize there was no chance in hell that the JCC presidential debate would go smoothly. Problem is, he allows his excellent morning and early afternoon to lure him into delusion.

SJ skips her classes for the day to help him get ready—which includes stopping him from using a cologne his dad gave him because she says it makes him smell like "a bribe-taking Supreme Court justice who used his privilege to escape a sexual assault charge."

They spritz something of Justyce's instead.

And though she and Justyce drill Jared to the point where he's sweating as they get him dressed, when he looks in the mirror—after Justyce has tied Jared's tie, straightened the lapels of his charcoal suit jacket, and tucked his blue patterned pocket square—Jared's impressed. He looks good.

But when all is said and done, Jared will be furious with himself for thinking his aesthetic would matter. He'll feel like an idiot for believing the stage arrangement—three podiums set in a slight arc, with him and Dylan on the ends and John Preston in the middle—put him at some sort of advantage. He'll smack his forehead over the way he smiles when he sees the diverse trio of moderators (Ari Park and the UCC's sitting VP and treasurer, a Mexican American girl and a white guy, respectively). And he'll hate that the sight of his friends—Justyce, SJ, Amir, Pat, Robbie, Roger, and Aaron—smiling up at him from the first row behind the moderators puts him at ease.

Worst of all, he's really gonna kick himself when he considers the way he just *relaxes* once he's knocked the first couple of questions out of the park (if the nods and thumbs-ups from his team are any indication). Because it makes him overconfident. And after speaking in favor of increased support for student-led organizations rooted in "affinity" markers—like ethnicity or sexual orientation—Jared aims a smile at Dylan.

Problem is, she doesn't see him—she's laser-focused on the moderators.

But John Preston LePlante IV sure does.

It's all downhill from there.

MODERATOR 1

Mr. Christensen, you seem to care a lot about student experience. How do you plan to ease the burdens felt by undervalued and underrepresented students on this campus?

JARED

Well, my plan is—

JOHN PRESTON

Might I take this one first?

The moderators all look at Jared like, *Well?*

JARED

Umm . . . I guess?

JOHN PRESTON

Great. This question contains a couple
of logical fallacies. First, nobody here
is "undervalued." Second, the group that
is *actually* underrepresented here is
white students. We make up over seventy-
five percent of the total US population,
but not even thirty-six percent of the
student population on this campus. In
contrast, Asian people make up around
seven percent of the total US population
but represent almost seventeen percent
of students here. And there are even
more international students—over twenty-
two percent. As such, the question as
you've asked it is unanswerable because
it suggests a false reality.

JARED

I—

DYLAN

If it's permissible, I would like to answer the question as it was asked.

MODERATOR 2

Go right ahead, Ms. Coleman.

DYLAN

Thank you. I'd first like to thank you for the rhetoric you chose, President Park. As a member of a racial group that makes up over thirteen percent of the U.S. population but less than seven percent of our student body here, I can assure you that there are many students from marginalized backgrounds who do feel overlooked and undervalued.

JOHN PRESTON

We're talking about facts, not *feelings—*

DYLAN
(acting like John Preston doesn't exist)

Since human beings are far more than demographic data, I think we start by asking these students what they need. Then we work to make sure they get it. The aim of a class representative should be hearing the concerns and representing the interests of as many members of the class as possible.

MODERATOR 3

(looking impressed)

Well said, Ms. Coleman. Next, we'd like to turn to a question based on language in your campaign, but we'd like to pose it to Mr. LePlante first.

John Preston stands up straighter, and Jared drops his chin so the moderators won't see him roll his eyes.

MODERATOR 3

Mr. LePlante, Ms. Coleman has proposed a one-course multicultural studies requirement in the undergraduate program. Do you think this would be beneficial to the student bod—

JOHN PRESTON

Absolutely not. In fact, when I'm elected president, *all* required "core" course hours will be abolished. As people who are paying to be here, students should be free to take whichever classes they please.

DYLAN

That doesn't really work at a regionally accredited university that offers specific degree programs. But go off, I guess.

A ripple of laughter echoes through the audience, and John Preston goes red-faced and grips the edges of his podium.

MODERATOR 1
(sensing the rising tensions in the room)

Mr. Christensen? Your thoughts?

JARED
(gulping)

Though I *do* recognize the necessity of required courses—proving one can do math as well as read and write in English *is* important—I worry that *adding* to this load could be burdensome to students—

JOHN PRESTON
Now he's talking like he's got some sense!

JARED
Dude, I'm not *agreeing* with you—

DYLAN
Except you *literally* are.

MODERATOR 3
What say you, Ms. Coleman?

DYLAN

People fight tooth and nail to get into
this school because of its reputation
for excellence. Considering our motto
is "Light and Truth," I think requiring
a sole single-semester course, aimed
at better preparing us to thrive in a
multicultural world, is fitting with the
ethos here.

MODERATOR 1
(openly smiling)

Very nice. Thank you.

MODERATOR 2

Final question, and anyone may—

JARED

Wait, can I respond to that?

MODERATOR 3

I'm sorry, Mr. Christensen, but we need
to move on.

JARED
(starting to crack)

Dude, I've gotten cut off four times—

JOHN PRESTON

Such is the nature of qood ol'-fashioned political debate in America, my friend.

DYLAN

That is resoundingly untrue from an historical perspective, but I think our *very* gracious moderators would like to move forward, if you gentlemen don't mind.

JOHN PRESTON

Is that *sycophancy* I hear, Ms. Coleman?

DYLAN

Don't use words you can't spell, booboo.

(to Moderator 2)

You were saying, Ms. Vice President?

Jared grips his podium to temper his rage, then feels himself turn red as it hits him how *alike* he and John Preston must look to the audience.

MODERATOR 2

(clearing her throat and fighting a smile)

Our final question: With the recent Supreme Court ruling against considerations of race on college applications, many are also calling for an end to legacy admissions. What say you?

JOHN PRESTON

No comment from me because this is moot. Legacy admissions have always been part and parcel to the continued greatness of this school, and there is absolutely no reason for that to change.

JARED
(perking up)

It's not *moot*. The concerns of every student have to be considered valid for the "greatness of this school" to carry forward.

DYLAN

That doesn't answer the question.

JARED
(fighting the urge to ask her to stop being mean . . . they're supposed to be on the same team!)

In answer to the question, I think that understanding HOW legacy factors into admissions is necessary before any decisions are made.

DYLAN

You still haven't answered the question.

JARED

(to Dylan)

Dude, what's your problem?

Dylan and Jared lock eyes, and the room goes so quiet, you could hear a mouse fart.

DYLAN

Both of your parents are alumni, aren't they, Mr. Christensen?

JARED

(blushing)

That is correct.

DYLAN

And your father is an alumnus as well, Mr. LePlante?

JOHN PRESTON

Father, grandfather, great-grandfather, and four uncles, to be exact.

DYLAN

How would you have felt if you hadn't gotten in, Mr. Christensen?

JARED

I mean, I did get deferred when I applied early . . .

DYLAN

And were you upset about that?

JOHN PRESTON

Is there a *point* to this Barbara Walters interview?

MODERATOR 3

Your lack of civility is anathema to this organization, Mr. LePlante. You are free to leave if you can't abide by the rules of engagement.

Jared doesn't hear the rest of the reprimand. He's too conscious of Justyce McAllister's and SJ Friedman's eyes on him. They were both present for his response to getting deferred. It's one of Jared's most shameful memories.

JARED

Yes, I was upset.

DYLAN

And yet here you are.
(beat)

What about you, Mr. LePlante? How would
you have felt if you hadn't gotten in?

JOHN PRESTON
(scoffing)

In a million years, that wouldn't have
happened.

DYLAN

It must've been nice to apply to a
college of this caliber with that much
confidence.

No one breathes.

DYLAN

Ending legacy admissions, which to
me means not letting "unqualified"
applicants in just because their parents
went here, is about making sure NO ONE
has an unfair advantage. If my race can't
be considered, the fact that Grandpa Ron
went here shouldn't be considered either.
If this institution intends to hold all
students to the same high standard, it's
gotta start at the application stage.

MODERATOR 1

And with that, we are out of time—

JOHN PRESTON

Wait, are you seriously letting her
conflate two *totally* different concepts—

JARED

Bro, will you just *shut up*?

MODERATOR 2

Y'all are dismissed. I gotta get outta here.

MODERATOR 1

Same.

DYLAN

*(walking past Jared on her way to
the exit)*

Great job, champ. Good luck at the
polls.

And now for a brief intermission.*

*This is the part where our discombobulated
antihero waltzes right into his old patterns
and makes a series of increasingly poor
decisions, including but not limited to:
heading straight to the frat house in his
suit (you know, for the Spring Sting party
he planned); downing every beverage handed
to him; giving Jell-O shots to known high
schoolers; setting off a bunch of fireworks
that were hidden in the frat house basement;
making a dry-ice bomb and throwing it into
the dumpster; kissing Ainsley Cruz on
sight (he felt REALLY bad about this one);
offering marijuana to the campus police,
who showed up to tell them to tone it down,
then playing it off as a joke; leaving the
house with an open tequila bottle in hand;
brazenly swigging from it on the street;
stealing a random bike, crashing it into
some bushes, and leaving it there; vomiting
beside a thankfully empty campus police car;
yelling at a cute couple canoodling on a
bench; taking another brazen swig from his
bottle and throwing his arms wide like a
court jester when they turned to look at him;
urinating somewhere that definitely wasn't
a bathroom; and apologizing profusely to
a tree.

He'll claim to "recognize the grave error" of his ways and to "know it's unlikely" that he'll "suffer any real consequences," and he'll also say he's "hyperaware of how messed up that is" and is "committed to doing better."

Guess we'll soon see . . .

ACT III

Winners and Losers

13

Upon Probable Cause

The silence inside Justyce's car is so dense, Jared's a thousand percent sure it's going to suffocate him. "Music," he groans, trying and failing to reach the knob for the radio.

"Oh, I know your ass is cooked if you think you 'bout to turn on *my* shit," Justyce says without taking his eyes off the road. "You know never to touch a Black man's radio, Jared!"

Jared sighs and lets his chin drop to his chest. "Sorry. Too quiet."

"You can deal," Justyce replies. "Besides, I can't risk turning something on and it throwing off your equilibrium. Because if you puke in my car, my inner Martin Luther King will take a seat, and good ol' Huey P. Newton is coming out, fists ready to fly."

Jared's stomach churns like *it's* ready to fly. "Point taken."

"We're almost home anyway," Justyce says. The air in the car shifts slightly, but Jared's too drunk to question it, even in his own mind. "You . . . uhh . . . got anything you wanna tell me?"

"Huh?" Jared opens his eyes and sees Justyce wringing the steering wheel. *Why does he seem nervous?*

"I mean, I'm sure you're gonna pass out cold once we get there. So, if you want to share anything about your night . . ."

Jared doesn't respond.

"Just saying now would be a good time. If you need to process anything."

Still nothing from Jared.

"You know . . . Like, any chance encounters?"

"Just need sleep," Jared replies, leaning his head back and closing his eyes.

Thing is, he's wide awake now. And far more sober than when Justyce dragged him off the base of the fountain outside the library and half-carried him to the car.

Because Jared *did* have a "chance" encounter. One that shook him up so bad, he finished off the bottle of tequila he'd taken from the frat house . . . then tried to make his way back there to grab another one.

The library was as far as he'd gotten. And shortly after arriving there (at least he *thinks* it was shortly . . .), he knew he'd reached the end of the road for the night. So he called his roommate, shared his location, slipped his phone into his pocket, and closed his eyes to drift into oblivion as he awaited rescue.

But oblivion is long gone now. Because if Justyce already knows about Jared's chance encounter . . . how many other people do?

*   *   *

It's not until Jared is in his room with the door closed that he feels safe enough to uncap the lid on his memory. During his drunken and aimless traipse across campus—in a *suit,* with an *open bottle* of liquor in hand, *right after* a live-streamed presidential debate . . . what the hell was he even *doing?*—he needed to pee real bad. So he stopped and did his business on a tree behind one of the residence halls, then apologized to said tree and gave it the best hug of its arboreal life.

Which would've been all well and good (probably) if he hadn't been spotted. And by the *worst* possible person.

"Jesus," came the voice from over his shoulder.

He was very much still hugging the tree . . . with the neck of the squat brown bottle clutched in his left hand. *And* his pants still undone.

"This might be a new low, even for you, Daddy's boy."

And when Jared turned around to meet her eyes—because he had to at least do *that,* didn't he?—Dylan Marie Coleman had her phone in her hand. And was recording. (He thinks.)

Jared was too stunned to speak.

"Wow, bro," came a second voice. Jared had been so focused on Dylan, he didn't notice she wasn't alone. "And here I thought *you* had more class than the typical rich white boys around here." Imani Williams (*from Constitutional Law,* some non-intoxicated part of his brain reminded him). She gave him a once-over and frowned. "No shade, but respect rescinded."

"I mean, at least he's not driving," came a third (!!!) voice. It was a girl Jared didn't recognize. Which gave him an odd sense of relief.

But then Dylan snorted. "Yeah, don't put it past him. It's *great* to be a white dude, ain't it, Jared? Drive drunk, piss on trees . . . How long you been walking around with that bottle in your hand? Has *anyone* tried to stop you?"

Jared didn't say a word. (The answer was no. No one had tried to stop him. Which even *he* is in disbelief about now. But it's true.)

Dylan just shook her head. "Presidential material, ladies and gentlemen." She lowered the phone and looked him in the eye, but he was too far gone to read her expression.

"Let's go, y'all," she said to her friends. And the three of them turned and vanished into the night.

Before he can give it too much thought, Jared heads over to his desk and opens his laptop.

A few nights prior, while essentially descending into madness after Dylan kept his apology voice note but didn't respond to it, Jared decided to poke around on the internet to see if he could learn more about her "unlawful wounding" felony.

After shelling out another small fortune to a different legal records website, he'd found the name of the alleged victim in the case: Marquis Jonathan Barry.

And he immediately shut his laptop.

Right now, though? Jared's gotta learn more about who he's dealing with. She took a *video* of him (again: he thinks). And Justyce clearly knows something's up . . . Has he *seen* it? What if she already posted it somewhere? Had she been live-streaming? How far has this gotten?

He clicks on a browser and looks the guy up.

The first thing Jared notices: The dude is *very* good-looking. He's a two-sport athlete at Dylan's former school, and Jared can see his positions—running back and power forward—as well as his stats. Similar build to Dionte: six-foot-four, 221 pounds of steel. He's featured in a digital roundup of "College Phenoms" on the ESPN website with his shirt off, and his abs are giving *brick wall.*

Which . . . *this* is the person Dylan Marie Coleman "unlawfully wounded"? Guy looks like he could crush her with a single bicep.

Before he can think too much about it, Jared pulls up one of Marquis's social media accounts, follows him, and then types up a direct message requesting a conversation.

It's a LONG shot through pitch-black darkness, and Jared knows it. Knows it as well as he knows he should just leave it all alone and let the chips fall where they may regarding this election. Maybe Jared *could* stand to "suffer some consequences for once," as SJ would put it. Also: Marquis Barry *surely* gets a crap ton of conversation-request messages and has zero reason to even *open* one from some random white boy in New England. Let alone respond.

But still: Jared taps the send button. (Because of course he does.)

Then, vaguely relieved, he shuts his laptop, takes off the suit he'll never be able to wear again—too many poor-choice memories embedded in the dark gray fabric—and gets into bed.

He's asleep before his head sinks into the pillow.

When Jared wakes to a response, he panics. Everything looks a little different when his brain isn't locked in the clutches of drunken paranoia. And despite feeling like his head has been impaled on a rusted railroad spike, Jared recognizes how creepy it was to message the guy in the middle of the night, asking if they could "chat."

Hence Marquis's reply catching Jared off guard:

> Yeah man we can chat.

> Looked you up and seen where you are and what you're doing and who your opponents are, so I'm pretty sure I know what you wanna chat about. Hit me at 11.

And there's a phone number.

Jared spends the next two hours going back and forth with himself about whether he'll use it. He hasn't gotten any emails or calls from the UCC, and the only person lighting up his message inbox is Ainsley (*Why did he kiss her last night?!*), so maybe Dylan *hasn't* attempted to force a reckoning . . .

(Jared still can't bring himself to talk to Justyce, but that's another matter.)

However, despite the lack of blowback, Jared's also sure Dylan is holding on to the evidence of his misdeeds. Because why wouldn't she? So at eleven o'clock on the dot, Jared taps out the number he maybe memorized and holds the device up to his ear.

It rings once . . . twice . . . three times . . . four . . .

He pulls it away and is about to hang up when "Hello?" comes through in a coarse half-whisper.

"Hello?" Jared says. "Is this Marquis?" (Jared says it like *mar-KWEESE*.) "This is Jared."

"Man, you white boys can't read a Black name to save your life. It's *MAR-kis*."

Shame washes over Jared, and he smacks his forehead. "Sorry about that, man."

"Nah, you good." And then the phone starts making a *boop*ing sound in Jared's ear. Marquis is requesting a video call.

It's a smidge more *intimate* than Jared was prepared for, but he answers. It's apparent that Marquis just woke up, but as he rubs the sleep from his eyes (and sheesh, this guy is *handsome*), he says, "Lemme guess, somebody busted the windows out your car."

"Wait, is that what she did to *you*?" Jared recalls the property damage charge.

"Nah, but I wouldn't put it past her," Marquis says. "She's definitely got a temper."

"We're talking about Dylan Marie Coleman, right?" Does Jared feel a little ridiculous asking this? Of course. But he has to make *sure,* doesn't he?

"Is that who you called me about?"

"Yeah."

"Well, then that's who we talkin' about, ain't it?" Marquis looks perturbed, but he keeps going. "Whatchu wanna know?"

"Oh. Umm . . . you were saying she has a temper?"

"Oh yeah. Absolutely." Marquis stares at Jared blankly.

"Do you . . . mind expounding?"

Marquis nods. "Got you. The long and short of it is: The girl you called about and I dated last year. Like *dated.* Non-exclusively. Aka, we weren't *together.* We weren't a couple."

Makes sense to Jared. He was in a similar situation with Ainsley. "Okay . . ."

"You see this scar?" Marquis holds the phone up to his neck, and Jared can see a faint line of shinier skin that stretches from just below his ear almost to his collarbone.

"Yeah."

"She got mad one night after she caught me with another girl," Marquis says.

Jared's heart starts beating faster. Part of him wants to end the call. Because despite the fact that he's getting exactly what he asked for—dirt on his opponent—this isn't lining up with the Dylan he knows. The one who said she'd taken down flyers from that stupid S.A.C.C.C.T.D.D. smear attempt and then checked (and double-checked!) to make sure he was okay. The one who reached out to *him* during *her* time of need and who slept in his arms because she said she felt safe there. And she ran up and threw her arms around him the night he was with his dad.

But that's also the night things took a turn. And Jared must admit: The girl he's been interacting with since is . . . different.

"She cut you?" he asks Marquis.

"Broke an heirloom vase that belonged to my dead grandma and sliced me with a piece of it."

Jared doesn't know what to say.

"She left *this* school to keep from getting expelled. And I stay pretty quiet about it because no need to dwell on the past," Marquis continues. "But yeah, you should know that bitch is crazy."

The pair of pejoratives ghost over Jared's skin and turn his stomach sour.

"She's also a liar, so don't bring this up to her. She's not gonna tell you the truth."

"Uhhh, okay . . ." *In what universe would he ask her about any of this?* Jared wonders.

"Just watch your back, all right?"

Jared hesitates. "Thanks, I guess . . ."

"Good luck with your election." And Marquis ends the call.

Jared stares at the screen until it goes dark. The pieces are all there: mug shot, criminal record, scar and story that match the charges, transfer to a new school . . . And yes, she hasn't exactly been *pleasant* over the past few days.

But still: Something doesn't *feel* right.

He's also not as . . . satisfied as he thought he'd be. Sure, if she tries to take him down, he has what he needs to hit her right back.

So why does he wish he could scratch the whole conversation with Marquis—including the guy's name—from his memory?

His phone pings in his hand, and he's shocked when he sees the name on the screen this time. It's a message from Dylan.

> Hey, totally forgot we scheduled a project meeting for this evening.

> I'm not really feeling up to it.

> We can finish up online.

Jared frowns. He forgot about the meeting too. And now he's sad it's not happening.

Because despite the way she's been treating him *and* everything he just learned, Jared still misses her.

14

Election of Representatives

When Jared's alarm goes off at 6:30 the next morning—on the day the polls are set to open—he yanks his phone off the charger and chucks it across the room.

Where it continues to blare.

He shoves his head beneath his pillow and groans.

As Dad advised when Jared was younger—*Choose the least pleasant sound you can find for an alarm so it jars you awake the way it needs to*—Jared chose the one that sounds like a screeching crow, and right now, each little *CAW! CAW!* is making him want to die.

His head feels on the brink of implosion, and he knows that the second he moves, his gut is going to swim, and he'll need to get to the trash can or toilet faster than he's sure he'll be able to.

"Fuuuuuu—"

There's a knock at the door. "J? You good in there, man?"

It's Justyce.

"Make it stop, please," Jared shouts.

The door opens, and Justyce comes in. Within seconds, the alarm has stopped, and the pillow is being lifted away. Jared cracks an eye. The overhead light is on—another brain stab—and Justyce is standing there with his hands in the pockets of his Nike tech fleece sweatpants, looking every bit like somebody's cool lawyer dad.

Kinda reminds Jared of Julian Rivers, Manny's father.

"What happened, dawg?" Justyce says.

"Ugh, no talky."

"Oh, yes talky, my friend." Now Justyce snatches the covers off. "The hell happened to you, man? Why do you look like you just lived through a damn zombie apocalypse? Didn't we *just* go through this the night *before* last? And what's this about the election being postponed?"

Jared sits bolt upright as though yanked by a string.

Which was a *terrible* idea. "WOW, that was . . ." His eyes go wide. "Trash can, please."

Justyce passes it to him. The contents of Jared's stomach promptly appear within.

"Should I . . . come back?" Justyce says then.

"Absolutely not." Jared hurls again and shuts his eyes. "Please don't leave me."

"Ohhh-kay."

Justyce pulls out the desk chair and takes a seat, and Jared, trash can still on the bed between his legs, massages his temples. For a beat, neither of them says anything.

Then: "Jus, I—"

"Lemme guess, actually," Jus cuts in. "Something not-great

happened last night—just like the night before—and you made a bad decision that's got the potential for nasty consequences."

Jared's stomach double-backflips into his throat. Which makes him want to puke again, but he's got nothing left. *Could Justyce know?* "What do you mean?" he says.

"Dawg, everything about this scenario is familiar to me," Justyce replies, looking around the room. "Remember that party your boy Blake Benson—"

"Definitely *not* my boy," Jared cuts in.

"Well, he was back then. Point being: He threw that party, I had far too much to drink, and the next thing I know, three white boys were saying I hit them."

"I mean, you did." Jared's jaw throbs at the memory.

"Oh, I believe you. Trust me. I definitely hit *something,* considering how swollen my hands were. Just don't remember that part," Jus continues. "Anyway, woke up the next morning feeling like the Grim Reaper had tried to French-kiss me. And then Doc showed up in my room. Kinda like I just popped up in yours."

"Weird." Jared breathes in and forces down another wave of vomit. He would really like to not talk anymore.

"Yeah. Wild to see the shoe on the other foot, or whatever that phrase is white people be sayin'," Justyce goes on. "So what'd you do this time? Pee on another sacred campus tree?"

So he *does* know about that. To Jared's surprise, however, in *this* moment, he doesn't really care why or how or if anyone else does.

Because Jared *did* make a bad decision last night that has the potential for some nasty consequences.

It all started innocuously enough: Yesterday morning, he'd

talked to the guy Dylan allegedly tried to murder (hyperboli-cally speaking) with a shard of his dead grandmother's antique vase. Shortly thereafter, Dylan canceled the project meeting they'd set more than a week prior. Then a few hours later—around two p.m.—he received notice that his frat was throwing an im-promptu Spring Sting 2.0 party that evening and his attendance was mandatory.

It initially made Jared feel pretty good: Even if Dylan hadn't canceled, the meeting would've needed to be rescheduled. Took the burn of her rejection down a hair. Was he thrilled about the "mandatory" bit? Definitely not. Especially considering the *previous* night's party and how all that turned out. (Like was it *really* necessary for the brothers to "run it back," as he'd heard Justyce say?)

His plan was to do what he typically did when Hunter re-quired party attendance: Pop in, make the rounds, and then slip out once the exec board members were too drunk to notice he'd left (which happened fairly quickly). Then he'd come back to the apartment and just go to bed. Sleep the day off and let his body reset for the biggest day of his college career so far: election day.

Except on his way across campus, who does he see on the quad but Dylan Marie Coleman? Who may not have been "feeling up to" meeting with him about the project that's worth a massive chunk of their Constitutional Law grade, but was perfectly fine to be out laughing and "keekee-ing" (as Jared once heard a Black girl say as she told her boyfriend off outside the student center) with one of the guys she'd humiliated Jared in front of.

It probably would've been fine if he'd managed to get past her without being seen. For one: The last time they saw each other had obviously been less than stellar. And for two: He really didn't want her to know he'd spotted her out and on a *date* or whatever.

It was too late for him to turn around without being noticed, so he pulled his baseball cap low, stuck his hands in his pockets, and lengthened his stride. His mistake had been failing to resist the urge to peek at them right as he passed where they were sitting.

The guy appeared to be whispering something in Dylan's ear, and she was giggling . . . but staring right at Jared. And when their eyes met, something inside Jared cracked.

Thus, Spring Sting 2.0 was almost as much of a blur as its predecessor. As soon as he got to the frat house—"No *suit* this time, Christensen?" a brother asked—he took a shot. Then he joined a game of beer pong. Then another two shots.

And though he doesn't remember much, he has a hazy recollection of somebody telling him they had his vote, and a different somebody mentioning "that Black girl" and how they "kinda dig some of her policy ideas."

He went and took another shot after that.

At some point, someone saw Jared—who was full-out wasted then—and cracked a joke about him making sure "not to get behind the wheel before the votes got counted." That launched a volley of commentary and questions about the S.A.C.C.T.D.D. smear campaign. Which just reminded Jared of his *chance encounter* at the tree the night before.

In his (again) drunken state, the facts hit him like a blow to the sternum: Dylan basically spilled his secret in front of her friends *and* potentially had video evidence of him blasted out of his gourd and desecrating a beloved campus mainstay.

So after seeing one of his frat brothers making out with a Black girl who had box braids (as Dylan told him they're called when the partitions make a girl's scalp look like a checkerboard), Jared downed another shot, pulled out his phone, changed the IP address to somewhere in Switzerland, then shot off an email to the UCC that included the mug shots he'd received as well as a screenshot and a link to Dylan's arrest record.

"Hellooooo?" Justyce is saying.

Jared snaps back to where he's sitting in bed, hugging a trash can full of liquid regret. "Huh?"

Justyce looks at Jared. Hard. Makes Jared feel like his skin is going to shatter and fall off. "Can you stop eyeballing me like you're trying to read my mind? You seeing me like this is bad enough—"

Jared's phone pings.

Justyce absentmindedly picks it up and looks at the screen, but his face gives nothing away. He passes the phone to Jared.

Even if he had anything left inside, he wouldn't be able to puke again. Because his stomach plummets from his throat to the floor beneath his bed.

It's a text from Dylan. And more are coming in.

Sorry for texting so early.

Not sure if you saw, but poll opening has been postponed without explanation.

Avis told me she heard LePlante got a couple warnings for "misuse of email" violations.

> Supposedly got a third violation for a campus-wide spam blast last night about voting for him.

> No surprise there.

> Anyway, just letting you know what I heard . . . And I guess wondering if you knew anything. Either way, hopefully it gets resolved soon.

"What she say?" Justyce asks, while Jared reads them again. (*Is the whole "Let's not acknowledge any of our recent trash interactions nor mention anything pertinent to what's going on between us" tactic something all girls do?* he wonders.)

He shakes his head clear. "She said she heard LePlante got a third violation for misuse of email."

"Ah, okay." Justyce nods. "So *that's* why the opening of the polls is delayed?" He looks Jared right in the eye.

And Jared knows he's gotta pull it together and never tell *anyone* what he did. After all the times Justyce has been there for Jared—sticking up for him and having his back and coming to his rescue and "holding space" for him as he tries (and frequently fails) to think and move differently—if Justyce *ever* found out what Jared did, he would instantly stop being his friend. Because this was too far. Even for Jared.

And Jared cannot lose Justyce. He *can't.*

So he gathers his inner politician and forces a shrug. "Dude, who even knows? The only *sure* thing is my dumb ass drank too much last night."

"Mm-hmm," Justyce replies. "Second night in a row."

Jared doesn't respond to that.

"Post-debate, I *kinda* got it," Justyce goes on. "Dylan handed you *and* that other white boy your asses, I mighta went and grabbed a drink too. But on the eve of the election? Bro, what's up with *that*? Haven't seen you party this hard since before that DUI."

Jared *could* tell the truth. At least partially. "Yeah, I know, man. Definitely made some choices I'm not super proud of," he says. "But I've been so *stressed* lately. Clearly need some better coping strategies—"

"This about Dylan?"

"Huh?" Welp, there goes Jared's game. "Naaah. Not even."

Justyce doesn't reply, so Jared looks at him. *And I'm the abominable snowman* is the message on Justyce's face.

"I mean . . . not entirely. She's a part of things, yes. But there's also like, schoolwork. And this election."

Justyce nods. "Well, for what it's worth, Dyl cares about you a lot."

Uhhh . . . "She does?" *And did Jus just call her Dyl like her friends do?*

"She does. The minute she left that tree, she called me. Said, 'Not to make you Captain Save-a-Ho, but your guy could definitely use your help.' And she sent me a video. Which she said she deleted after it showed 'delivered.'"

So she *had* been recording—

Wait . . . Dylan *called* him? "She has your number?"

"Yeaaah, about that . . . ," Justyce replies. "I've known Dyl since she first started here. Was the orientation leader for her transfer group. Truly incredible young lady."

Jared's mouth drops. "You mean this *whole time*—?"

Justyce raises his hands. "Hey, I mind my business, man. Anyway, hopefully they get things sorted and open the polls. It's out of your hands now," he says. "So get back on that horse. You've been doing too well to return to the old ways."

This makes Jared smile. "I appreciate that, man."

Justyce stands and, before Jared can protest, grabs the trash can of sick. "I'm dumping this," he says. "Get up and pull yourself together, yeah?"

Jared's chin drops as his facade falls away. He hates how good a friend Justyce is being. If only he knew . . .

"Hopefully what Dyl told you about John Preston is true," Justyce says as he heads to the door.

He eyeballs Jared again, and Jared instantly deflects. "All *I* know is that I want this election to be over."

April 19

Dear Manny,

So . . . I'm not gonna drag this out, and I'll try to be as forthright as possible . . . something I'll admit I HAVEN'T been with very many people over the past week. I did something really messed up. And now I have to sit with the results of my actions while also staying the course AND making sure no one finds out it was me.

Long story short, the opening of the polls got pushed back 24 hours, and there will only be two names on the ballot: mine and John Preston LePlante IV. The email that went out to everyone was vague: "Attention, junior class voters: Due to a technicality, Dylan Marie Coleman's candidacy has been rescinded, and her name will not appear on the final ballot. Apologies for any inconvenience."

The announcement went out at around one p.m. . . . four hours after the polls were originally set to open. I overheard people talking about it as I walked around campus, and for the most part, everyone seems to believe that the "technicality" has something to do with her being a transfer student. Which was actually a huge relief. Now that I'm back sober and have seen the light of day, I don't want anyone to know Dylan's secret. (If you ever see me drinking that much again, please haunt the hell out of me.)

The other thing, though—and this feels like a confession, so it has to stay between us—I'm also relieved that she's out of the race. There was a US presidential election recently—the first one I got to vote in—where neither of the major party candidates were *ideal*, but one seemed almost anti-democracy. Then this third-party candidate announced intent to run, and people freaked out . . . Which is something

155

I didn't understand until now: The people who are going to vote for John Preston aren't likely to be swayed to my or Dylan's side, but if Dyl and I wound up splitting the other votes, it would increase John Preston's chances of being elected.

Aka, with Dylan out, *I* have a better chance of winning.

There. I said it.

However . . .

I *really* messed up, Manny. I honestly don't know what I was thinking.

Actually, I WASN'T thinking. That's the problem. I got jealous and paranoid, and I did a stupid, stupid thing without giving any thought to the consequences.

And I'll probably get away with it.

That's the part that's really eating at me. Today, I heard Justyce talking and laughing on the tail end of a video call as I was headed to the kitchen. It was your cousin Quan. When Jus hung up, he just looked so *happy*. I asked what was going on, and he told me Quan got into this super hardcore math program at Georgia Tech. He'll be starting there in the fall. "Do you have any idea how HUGE this is, Jared?" He looked like he was about to explode from excitement.

I really *didn't* have any idea, but I smiled anyway. Jus being that happy made *me* happy, and the thought of Quan going to college was awesome.

"Bruh, we're talking about a kid who'd basically given up," Justyce continued. "Dude sat locked up for two and a half YEARS over something he didn't do, and all because he couldn't see a different path for himself. And now he's going to one of the top STEM schools in the world." He shook his head and let it drop.

And when Jus looked back up, he was crying.

"Sorry for getting all emotional, but DAMN, man!" he said. "To go from feeling like people look at you and see nothing but some menace to society to realizing you got the juice to go to COLLEGE?" He shook his head. "I know higher education was never NOT an option for you, so my emotionality may not make sense. But trust me when I say this is a big-ass deal."

That's when a lump formed in MY throat. Because Jus was right, Manny: I really didn't get it. I couldn't.

That's when the weight of what I'd done—and more importantly, why I'd been able to do it AND get away with it—dropped down on me hard. And I remembered, Manny. I remembered how pissed I was at you after we got in that stupid fight. I was so angry that you weren't laughing at my jokes anymore. That you seemed to be taking them so much more seriously than you did before. I hated that it felt like Justyce was getting in your head and you were becoming this whole other person. You'd been my best friend and closest confidant since second grade. And you were never "Black" to me. You were just . . . Manny.

But THAT Manny was disappearing, and I was so damn mad about it.

I couldn't take it, man. I couldn't take the fact that you were changing. That you were no longer the Manny *I* knew and depended on. I couldn't take the fact that you suddenly seemed to be on Justyce's side, and that you'd started to see and believe things about me that I didn't want to admit were true.

So I did what I knew I could do to get back at you. I told my dad I wanted to press charges. I've never admitted that to anyone, Manny. I've never told anyone that it was ME.

My dad only did it because I asked him to. He even asked if I was sure. "You boys have been friends for a long time, Jared." And I said

I didn't care. I took my frustrations about a bunch of shit I couldn't control, and I dumped them on our friendship. I can see that clearly now.

And then you died.

Now here I am again.

The WORST part about all of this? I'm gonna let things play out. Because I CAN, Manny. People looked at your cousin and saw a menace to society, but they look at me and they see a leader. That's just how my dad raised me. Could I do the "right" thing here and come forward about those DUI allegations being true? I could. Could I admit to Dylan that I'm the reason she got booted from the race? (At least I think I am . . . they didn't exactly confirm the nature of the "technicality," so I can't say for 100% sure.) I could. Could I rescind my candidacy on the grounds that I've broken campaign rules? I could.

But I won't. Why? Because I don't have to. That's what I've come to recognize.

I would never, ever admit any of this to anyone who could repeat it, but now that all the chips have fallen, there are a bunch of things I can see clearly:

1. I work super hard. I really do. BUT I really <u>don't</u> have the same stuff working against me as Dylan or Justyce (or any other Black student).

2. I don't HAVE to "prove" that I'm worthy of being at this school.

3. I don't HAVE to get good grades and avoid getting kicked out, because I know that no matter what my dad says, he's not actually going to let me fail.

4. I don't HAVE to be honest or upstanding or kind or even concerned with whether people "like" me or not.

There are obviously limits. But in so many ways, I can do and be and move however I want to, man. And though there's a part of me that recognizes how messed up that is, there's another part that says, "Why the hell would I give that up?"

There's really no point to this letter. Guess I'm just reckoning with it all. After writing it out, I'm kind of . . . numb.

Gonna go shoot some hoops, I think. Blow off some steam.

Thanks for listening, I guess.

—Jared

15

Witness Against Himself

At 8:30 the following evening—half an hour before the election polls close—Jared is in the basement rec room at the fraternity house reading the newspaper when he hears footsteps on the stairs behind him.

"Knock, knock," comes a girl's voice (complete with a literal knock on the wall).

Jared turns and almost falls off the couch. "Avis?"

"In the flesh." She strides over and plops down beside him as she looks around. The dimly lit room has plush green carpet, oak-paneled walls, and oversized brown leather furniture in addition to a pair of pool tables. "It's wild how even when *not* filled with intoxicated underage coeds, this room still looks like a den of iniquity," she says.

Jared . . . doesn't really know how to respond. For one, the *last* person he'd expect to waltz into a restricted area of his fraternity house is the campaign manager of the girl he got kicked out of the race (he thinks). For two, he has no idea—

"You're wondering how the hell I got in here?" She snatches the thought right out of his head.

"Uhhh . . . kinda?"

"And also what I'm doing here?"

Again, Jared doesn't say anything.

She nods. "Got it. So, to the first question: I've been to a few parties here, and a good handful of your 'brothers' have given me their 'business cards'—after expressing that they 'have a thing for Asian girls,' of course—and told me to 'reach out' if I 'ever need anything,'" she says. "Is it outlandish to act as though a college and major qualify as an occupation? Indubitably. But I was looking for you, and Amir said you were here. So I poked one of them for assistance."

"Ah."

"Don't think he loved that *you* were who I asked about when he let me in, but oh well. Here we are."

"Indeed," Jared replies.

"And to why we're here . . ."

She pauses. Waits for him to look her in the eye.

"I know it was you," she says.

Jared opens his mouth, but nothing comes out.

"Background first," Avis continues. "Dylan and I have been best friends since fourth grade. I was the new kid at the super-white, all-girls Catholic school we went to back home. My first day there, she brought her cute self over to weirdo me and said,

'I know you're new and probably scared, but I'm going to be your best friend, okay? We can be different together.' Stole my heart right then and there."

"Wow." Manny had done something similar when Jared was new in second grade. "That's kind of amazing."

"Correct. So imagine my horror when my bestie called me sobbing yesterday and said the UCC found out about a bogus criminal charge from her old school, and she'd been disqualified from the race."

Jared's back to not saying anything.

"She said she tried to explain that the charges were being dropped and her expungement was pending. But they cited the contract she'd signed and hit her with a 'Be that as it may, you didn't disclose this information.'"

She lets Jared sit in that for a sec.

"Right. So *I* asked if *she'd* asked how they found out, and *she* said *they* said they'd received an anonymous tip."

Still not a word from Jared.

"Now with *her,* you're in the clear—"

"Huh?" Jared's head snaps in Avis's direction.

"Dyl is convinced that the guy involved in the case is watching her online and sent them the information when he saw that she was running."

"Huh," from Jared.

"However, though that's feasible, something about it didn't sit right with me," she continues. "Not that I have the heart to tell her this, but I met the guy once when I went to visit her, and I could instantly tell that if you're out of his sight, you're out of his mind."

"That's kinda harsh. . . ."

"Truth hurts sometimes. Anyway, I decided to do some digging of my own. Long story short, I located an email sent to the UCC two nights ago, and when I traced the origin, the initial IP address said Switzerland. But it took me all of six seconds to get past that, and what did I find? The *real* IP address . . . which I geolocated to this very house. I'm a computer science major, by the way."

Jared clenches his teeth to keep his mouth from falling open.

"So I'm thinking one of your brothers has it in for my girl . . . but then I looked at the online record attached to the email. When I hacked into the account that had procured it, whose name did I see on the credit card used for membership dues?"

Jared's chin drops to his chest. He really is caught.

"I'm not gonna tell her," Avis says then.

It takes the words a second to register in Jared's brain. "Wait . . . ," he says. "Really?"

"Really. For one, it would crush her," Avis replies. "Also, I feel like leaving that particular ball in *your* court is the better move. For reasons I can't *begin* to fathom"—she looks Jared over and scrunches her nose—"she seems to really like you, Jared."

Jared is flabbergasted. "She *does*?"

"That incident with your dad notwithstanding. Actually, what the hell *was* that? Did you really just *stand* there?"

Jared shakes his head. "Not my proudest moment, I can assure you."

"Well, that aside, you're low-key all she's been talking about over the past few weeks. You're apparently 'sweet' and 'earnest' and 'a total gentleman'?" She scrunches her nose again. "Anyway, she's been super worried."

"Worried? About what?" Jared hasn't been this confused since he had a thing for Liberty Ayers, the African American social work intern he worked on Manny's cousin Quan's case with. And it turns out she doesn't date guys.

"Well, as of a few nights ago, she's been worried about your well-being." Avis looks at him. "You really peed on the sacred tree?"

"Can we not, please?"

"Too soon?" Avis puts a mocking hand over her heart. "Fine. You're never living that down, though. Anyhoo, before that, she worried you'd get the wrong idea about why *she's* been distant. And that you'd give up on her."

"Oh," Jared says.

"And after talking to Amir about you, I really do think you're a decent guy, even if you *are* an idiot. So I'm going to tell you what she can't, and then *you* get to decide if you're gonna tell her what you did."

Jared can't believe he's asking this, but: "Is she okay with you telling me her business?"

"She's the one who asked me to do it."

Interesting. "And she can't tell me herself because—"

"She's under an NDA."

"Got it." Jared certainly doesn't have anything to say to that.

"Short version: Last year, Dylan was assaulted by this hotshot athlete at her old school. She told a series of so-called authority figures there, but no one would do anything about it. Kept asking her for *proof.*"

Jared can't even open his mouth. Might unleash the fires of hell if he does.

Avis goes on. "So, one night, our girl decides to go to this guy's apartment. Try to get him to confess while she's secretly recording." She shakes her head. "I tried to talk her out of it, but her childhood crime-show obsession seemed to be manifesting in a private-eye delusion.

"She gets there, and the guy's got another girl inside, but he invites Dylan in anyway. Details here are murky, but from what I understand, he tried to talk her into joining the little party he was already having with this other girl, who was mostly undressed. When Dylan said no and tried to leave, he wouldn't let her. There was a struggle, and a vase fell and broke. And when he overpowered Dylan, wrestled her to the floor, and tried to undo her pants, she grabbed a shard and cut him with it."

The more Avis talks, the more Jared feels like the very roots of his existence are disintegrating.

"Dyl was able to get out of there, but the guy called the cops and had charges filed against her. And the other girl who was there backed up his story."

"That's . . . wow."

"Yeah. Thing is, when the cops found out she'd filed that assault complaint against him with the school, it muddied the waters. They said that to move forward with the charges against Dylan, they'd also have to investigate *those* claims. And the school didn't want that. So they told Dyl they would have the charges dropped AND pay her a small settlement provided she signed an NDA and left the school. So that's what she did."

If Jared could dissolve into the green carpet right now, he would.

"Except it's been like eight months, and they haven't followed through. Her parents hired a new lawyer recently, so hopefully it'll all be water under the bridge soon. In fact, that guy you saw Dyl with the night you guys were supposed to meet for your project—"

"Wow, she really does tell you *everything*," Jared says.

"She's my bestie. The lawyer is that guy's mom."

Jared knows his face has turned sour. "Ah."

"She's not into him at all, by the way. She told him so as soon as you disappeared from the quad."

Jared nods. It's a lot to take in.

And now a lot to process.

Even if Dylan *does* "really like" him, there are complications, aren't there? She hasn't been very nice to him as of late, and even though he can understand why, the fact remains that he *did* apologize about the situation with his dad. Was there something more he was supposed to do?

And then, of course, whether Avis tells her or not, Jared *did* get Dylan kicked out of the race. Even if she never finds out it was him, *he* will always know. And he's not sure he'd be able to live with that sort of beluga whale swimming around in his brain.

"Polls close in five minutes," Avis says, looking at her watch. "And I gotta jet because I have a date at nine-oh-one p.m."

"That's rather specific," Jared replies.

"Yes. Well, when you're a campaign manager who has the hots

for your candidate's opponent's campaign manager, you can't *really* date until the election's over. 'Conflict of interest' or what have you."

Jared can't help but smile then. He may have shot *his* chances to hell, but at least Amir's getting the girl. "I'll walk you out," he says.

On their way, Avis has to go to the bathroom. It's across from the frat president's office, so he leans on that doorframe as he waits for her to come out. Which is when he sees a stack of papers that were hastily tossed into the trash can. For a second, he's pretty sure his heart is no longer beating. He's staring, dumbfounded, as she comes out.

"All right, all done," she says, bringing him back.

They walk out to the porch, and she looks at her watch. "Nine-oh-four," she says. "I'm late."

"Ah, A.T. will be fine. I'll tell him it's my fault."

Avis smiles. "You're annoying and still have a *lot* of internal work to do, Jared Christensen. But I genuinely hope you win this thing."

"Odd coming from you, considering all you know, but I'll take it, Ms. Johnson."

"If you ever mention this to anyone, I'll deny it *and* tell everyone what you did, but between the two of us, I'm glad Dylan got knocked out of it. She showed up here wanting to *prove* she's got the juice, but my honey bun's got some healing to do. I think this whole thing woke her up to that reality."

"I should've been disqualified too" is Jared's response.

"Oh, I know," she replies. "Amir told me a while ago."

Jared stands dumbfounded as she heads to the sidewalk. Amir *told* her?

"Don't be mad at him, okay?" she says, looking over her shoulder. "He was feeling conflicted after that whole S.A.C.C.C.T.D.D. thing, and I'm easy to talk to. You're still the best hope we've got, and anyone with half a brain knows it. See ya!"

She heads down the hill and disappears into the night.

16

Abuses and Usurpations

When Hunter Landis comes into the frat president's office the following morning and sees Jared Peter Christensen sitting in his chair with his feet propped up on the desk, Hunter turns red so fast, Jared wonders if he's going to spontaneously combust.

Shortly after polls closed last night, a message went out from the UCC:

We, the Executive Board of the Undergraduate College Council, sincerely appreciate the willful exercise of your collegiate civic duty through the act of voting in our elections.

Due to the shift in our election day—from Friday to Saturday—results will be announced on Monday morning.

When it hit Jared that he'd have to wait thirty-six hours to learn if he'd won, he genuinely wondered if he would survive the weekend. But then he went to the kitchen for a snack and saw a note on the house whiteboard: Hunter would be off-campus until the next morning. So Jared decided to investigate that thing he'd caught sight of in his frat president's trash can.

S.A.C.C.C.T.D.D. flyers.

Loads of them. Ones that were printed but never distributed.

Jared was sad about it at first. In truth, he'd wanted to be wrong. But shock turned to disappointment turned to fury turned to acceptance. Now here he is, enjoying every last ounce of Hunter's apparent befuddlement.

"Something I can help you with, Jared?" the older boy says, trying to recover himself and reassert his authority.

Jared kicks the stack of flyers off the desk, and they spread across the floor. Right into Hunter's line of sight.

"Ah" is all he says.

"I honestly didn't want to believe it." Jared leans back. "I was passing by this office last night, and I saw those in your trash can, but I thought, *no way*. Couldn't possibly be!"

Hunter shoves his hands into the pockets of his chino shorts and lifts his chin. Instantly reminds Jared of that Morgan girl and her air of entitled defiance in the face of confirmed wrongdoing. It disgusts him.

"I just wanna know why, man," Jared says. "You constantly talk about how members of this organization are 'bred for leadership,' but then I pursue a major leadership position and you try to sabotage me? What kind of leadership example is that?"

"You know what your problem is, Christensen?"

Jared spreads his arms like *Do tell.*

"You've got your head so far up your own ass, all you can see is your insides."

Jared's face scrunches in confusion . . . because it's a terrible metaphor. Hunter, though, seems to take the look as Jared being dense and needing further explanation.

"You're never here, bro," he goes on. "You show up when you're obligated to, then you go back to living your little liberal lifestyle."

Ah. Of course that's what this is about.

"I knew something was awry when you decided you were going to live with that Black kid instead of moving into the house," Hunter says. "The guys were bugging me about it for weeks. *Dude, Christensen's dad's paid for a whole remodel, and he doesn't even live here?*"

Jared nods. "All right. Duly noted. Go on."

Hunter looks taken aback but continues. "When your so-called *campaign* went live and we all saw the changes you wanted to make?" He shrugs and leans against the door. "You had to be stopped, man."

"And how do you think good ol' Bill Christensen is gonna feel about you trying to ruin his son's reputation on this campus?"

Hunter's neck goes red. "Excuse me?"

"Do you have any idea how hard my dad's lawyers worked to

get all record of that DUI scrubbed clean? How much *money* he spent?"

The red creeps up from Hunter's neck into his jaw and lower face. "Dude, you're being extreme," he says, panic edging into his voice. "We tried to get you kicked out of an election, not ruin your reputation—"

"Are you under the impression that spreading rumors around campus made people gaze upon me with admiration?"

The red reaches Hunter's hairline, and he doesn't respond this time.

So Jared just stares. And Hunter stares back.

Then Hunter smiles. "You think you're so big and bad now, huh? Gonna run and tell Daddy that mean old Hunter tried to poop on your little presidential run? You don't have what it takes to be a leader, Jared. You're pathetic. So easily swayed by the sob stories of people who could never be as great as you could be. We're *better* than them, Jared. Point blank, period—"

"You know 'point blank, period' has its origin in African American Vernacular English, right?"

That seems to push Hunter over the edge. "You need to leave," he says. "You don't belong here. Nothing you say or do represents this organization well. We value *hard work* and *responsibility*, not handouts or handholding. *Merit* and *excellence*, not participation trophies and mediocrity. *Tradition* and *preservation*, not—"

"I'm fully aware of what the 'values' are, Hunter."

"You sure don't act like it. You're a scourge on this fraternity, and I fully intend to let your dear ol' dad know as much."

And in that moment, something hits Jared harder than Dylan's rejection did: When Jared looks at and despises Hunter Landis . . . he's really seeing himself.

Well . . . sort of. They're not *exactly* the same, but Jared can certainly see some unpleasant similarities. What Jared said to that Morgan girl—and the demoralizing way he said it—comes to mind.

The moment he heard Manny had been killed, Jared's eyes popped open to a reality he'd fought to deny: People *absolutely* viewed him and his best friend differently based solely on their skin colors.

But had he *done* anything about it? Was he doing anything about it now? Yeah, he'd run for Junior Class Council president and *claimed* he wanted to make this campus a more comfortable place for the students who don't have the same access to resources that he does (through no fault of their own). But he'd also pushed back against some of Dylan's proposed policies because they seemed "too radical"—as though big change doesn't require actual big changes.

Jared stares at Hunter, knowing that the only reason he's still sitting here—still *able* to sit here in a chair behind the desk of his fraternity president after blatantly disrespecting the guy by kicking a stack of flyers onto the floor—is because Dad literally *paid* for his ability to do so.

Which makes something else click: In this moment, Jared is utilizing that power to defy the type of guy he's *sure* would've blamed his dead best friend for his own death.

It feels pretty damn good. Maybe *this* is the way?

"You know what?" Jared says, standing up and walking over to

Hunter, stepping on S.A.C.C.T.D.D. flyers as he goes. It's only now that Jared realizes how much shorter his frat president is: The guy is eye-level with Jared's Adam's apple.

"You can tell my dad whatever you want," Jared says, deliberately looking down his nose. "He may very well choose you over me. But there *is* one thing I know for sure . . ."

"What's that?"

"You and he are prime examples of men I never want to be."

Hunter's face goes white with rage. Jared finds it oddly satisfying.

"Now, if you'll excuse me, I have my own presidency to prepare for." He steps into the hallway and strides toward the exit with more confidence than he's felt in years.

He is a Christensen, after all, and that *does* carry weight around here.

Time for him to do something with it.

17

Governments Long Established

At 8:03 a.m. on Monday, there's a knock on Jared's bedroom door.

He really doesn't want to answer. Too awash in regret.

His phone pings. And pings again. Then it rings.

More knocking. "I know you're in there, bruh. Can I come in?" Justyce says through the thick wood.

Jared flips onto his stomach and puts the pillow over his head.

The only thing louder than his chiming phone and the incessant knocking of his endlessly patient roommate are his final words to Hunter Landis, blasting through his head as though shouted through a bullhorn: *Now, if you'll excuse me, I have my own presidency to prepare for.*

Four minutes ago, Jared found out his statement had been false. He did *not*, in fact, have a presidency to prepare for.

Because he lost.

John Preston LePlante IV, crown prince of assholes, won the JCC presidential election.

He flips onto his back and moves the pillow to his midsection. Not caring at all now that he's wrinkling the periwinkle button-down shirt he painstakingly ironed to record the victory speech that's due at ten a.m.

He *lost* the election. To a guy who has zero qualms about tossing their campus back to 1869—the year before the first Black student was permitted to officially enroll as an undergrad.

But *how?* Had Hunter's smear campaign worked? Are there really *that* many people in their class who agree with John Preston's ideas?

The loudest question of all, though: Would Dylan have won if he hadn't gotten her booted?

"I'm coming in, man. If you're naked, cover up," Justyce says.

Jared hears the door open, but his eyes stay fixed on the ceiling.

"Damn, bro, you got your shoes on the *bed?*" Justyce says. It's so unexpected, Jared shifts his focus to his roommate. Jus is shaking his head. "Just wild. I mean, *no* kinda home training."

Jared can feel a giggle bubbling in his chest, and even though he'd absolutely prefer to wallow in stunned disbelief at his situation (*He lost?!*), the laughter bursts out of him.

Then Justyce is laughing too. He comes over and smacks Jared's calf. "Sit your uncouth ass up, man," he says.

Jared complies, swinging his legs over the edge of the bed, and Justyce sits down beside him. As their laughter dies and they settle into the weighty silence, Jared is thrown back to a moment he'll never forget:

"Remember that time we bumped into each other at Manny's grave?" he says to Justyce.

Who snorts. "How could I forget?"

"Why were you so nice to me?"

The question seems to catch Justyce off guard. "Whatchu mean?"

"I'd been such an *ass*," Jared says. "Honestly, in a lot of ways, I feel like Manny's death was my fault—"

"Nah, don't go there, man. There were hella contextual *and* societal factors involved in Manny's murder, but the only person who truly *caused* his death was the man who pulled the trigger."

Jared sighs. "I hear that, Justyce. I do. But I still feel like I bear *some* responsibility."

"False guilt will eat you alive, Jared. Trust me. You gotta let that go."

Should he tell Justyce the truth? Might as well . . .

"I really do, though, Justyce. I know everyone heard it was my dad who decided to press charges. But . . ." He takes a deep breath. "Well, the idea came from me. I *asked* him to do it."

Justyce is silent.

Jared goes on. "I . . . uhh . . . also got Dylan kicked out of the race."

Now Justyce turns to face Jared. "You *what?*"

"I know, I know." Jared puts his head in his hands. "Come to think of it, me losing is probably karma—"

"Miss me with the rationalizing, Jared. It's already taking a *lot* of willpower not to punch you in the mouth. So tread lightly."

Jared puts his hands up. "Heard, understood, and totally justified. But that's exactly my point: I've been an asshole. Without

177

question. And I was even *worse* back when we ran into each other at the cemetery."

It's quiet for a moment, then Justyce says, "I hope you're not waiting for a rebuttal."

"Nah. Just letting it sink in. I saw a therapist for a couple months after Manny died, and he stressed the importance of 'sitting in uncomfortable truths.' Just hadn't taken the advice until now, I guess."

"Meanwhile, I gotta *live* in them. Must be nice to have a choice in the matter."

More quiet, because there's nothing Jared can say to that, and then: "I really do want to know why you were nice."

"I wasn't nice," Justyce says. "I was kind."

"Is there a difference?"

"Hell yeah, there's a difference. I spent my whole life being *nice,* man. Creating minimal waves and working hard to make sure everyone around me was comfortable. That's what I was *told* would keep me safe," Justyce says. "All that went out the window when me and Manny got shot.

"My *kindness,* though? That's a *choice.* I know who I am, how I feel, and what I'm about, so I make my decisions based on the type of person *I* want to be. Because the only person I *gotta* spend the rest of my life with is me."

"Damn," Jared replies. "That's deep."

"I really hated you, man," Justyce says. "I hated you more than I've ever hated anybody. But that day at that gravesite, two things came to mind. The first was something Manny's dad said after you made that foul ass slavery 'joke,' and Manny justifiably beat the brakes off you."

Justyce pauses to let that land, and Jared bites his tongue (as he knows he should).

"Mr. Rivers was telling us about how he overheard one of his white subordinates call him a racial slur, but he didn't fire the guy. 'People often learn more from getting an undeserved pass than they would from being punished,' is what he said. Those words popped into my head as I read the engraving on Manny's headstone while standing next to you."

"That stings, but also makes sense," Jared replies.

"And then I also thought about my Dr. King journal. And I asked myself not only what Martin would do, but what Manny would want."

Jared nods. He knew that part.

There's really no more to be said.

Justyce gets up and punches Jared in the shoulder. It's a *bit* harder than friendly, but Jared's felt the full force of Justyce's fists and knows his friend—the best friend he has—is exercising immense restraint. He's thankful.

"Don't sit in here moping," Jus says. "It'd be a waste of them nice clothes you put on."

As soon as he's out the door, Jared's phone *tings!* A very specific sound that lets him know he's gotten an email from Dylan.

He grabs it and taps the notification on the screen before he can think too much about it. Subject line is "For your approval."

It's a link to their completed Constitutional Law project.

And it's immaculate. Far better than Jared could've pulled off on his own. Their "candidate's" platform and position on the issues they chose is so well articulated that, if he didn't know better, he'd be fully convinced he was reading through the campaign of a GOP nominee for president of the United States.

He shakes his head in shame. Dylan Marie Coleman had zero issue engaging with and articulating views that run totally counter to her own. And Jared hasn't even figured his out yet.

He decides to give her a call. There are so many things he needs to confess to her. So much to make amends for.

She doesn't answer. So he swallows his pride and records a voicemail: "Hey, Dylan. Got the project. It's . . . wow. Yeah, you really crushed it. So thankful you were assigned to be my partner . . . though I doubt you feel the same. Ha! Anyway, call me back when you get a chance. I'd like to talk to you about a few things. Thanks again, and talk to you soon. Hopefully."

He goes quiet, and after a few beats, an automated voice kicks in: *If you have finished recording, you can hang up to deliver the message, or press one to re-record—*

Jared pulls the phone away from his ear and presses one.

The voice pours out of the receiver again: *At the tone, please record your message—*

He hangs up. Then smacks his forehead.

His phone *pings!* this time. Incoming text.

Can't talk at the mo.

Hope the project is okay?

The normalness of the messages makes Jared want to cry. Because he knows—*knows!*—especially after talking to Justyce, that he doesn't deserve a response at all.

Jared sighs and decides to scan through his other messages. There's a series of loooooong texts from Amir that are very *pick up that chin, we're running again next year and we're gonna WIN it!* There are a handful of *Sorry, pal* messages in a group text from Pat, Robbie, Roger, and Aaron. There are clearly compulsory consolation texts from a few of his frat brothers (he guesses Hunter decided against making him an enemy of the house?), and there's even a message from Ainsley about how "appalled" she is that John Preston won and how she *cannot believe the majority of our class voted against the best interests of themselves and posterity.*

That last one makes him chuckle and shake his head (*Why are girls so confusing?*), but none of the messages are helping. He's got a black hole the size of Texas in his chest.

As Jared sits and allows his defeat to wash over him, he recognizes that the hole isn't from losing the election (though, yes: that's certainly burning at the edges). Will Dad be disappointed? Likely. Especially if Hunter makes good on his snitching. Justyce was definitely disappointed, and he knows Dylan will be too, once he tells her the truth. She may never speak to him again, which is something he'll have to get okay with.

But still. The hole is *him.* No matter who else is disappointed, it's nothing compared to the disgust Jared has toward himself, and the emptiness he feels over not really *knowing* who he is or what he's about.

Something Justyce said echoes in Jared's mind: *The only person I gotta spend the rest of my life with is me.*

Jared catches sight of himself in the full-length mirror that hangs on the back of his door. It was nailed there when he and

Justyce moved in, and Jared uses it every day without thought, but it never occurred to him how amazing it is to be able to look at himself by choice.

Is the boy—well, *man*, really (ish)—staring back at him someone he can live with for the rest of his life?

He gets off the bed and walks over to his reflection. Gives himself a good look.

Jared Peter Christensen honestly has no idea who he is.

But he smiles anyway. He'll figure it out.

And once he does, he's determined to *like* who he sees.

April 27

Dear Jared,

First, let's address the obvious: Is it weird to be writing a letter to myself? Absolutely. But as *woowoo* (and therefore absurd) as it seems, it also feels necessary.

Second: Know that this was not my idea. I've recently discovered that most of the "good ideas" I have and the things I do that change me in some way don't typically originate with me. Historically, I've not only taken credit for them, but have also genuinely believed myself when I've claimed someone else's genius as my own. The one exception is when I told Justyce and SJ we should try to help Manny's cousin Quan get out of jail (legally, of course). That idea truly did come from me. (Us?)

Anyway, the idea to write this letter came from Dylan Marie Coleman. Though I waited until after she'd submitted her non-rescindable evaluation of my performance on our project, I eventually told her that I was the "anonymous tip" giver who got her booted from the race. As it turns out, my intuition was correct when I asked Justyce to be close by but out of sight, because unlike him, she did not keep herself from punching me in the mouth. In fact, she tackled me, sat on my chest, and whaled on me until Justyce managed to pull her off. (Shout-out to the black eye, bruised jaw, and busted lip she left as mementos.)

A few days later, she reached out and asked if we could meet. And after she gave me her word that the urge to maim/murder/beat me to a pulp had passed, I agreed. We met in the café where we'd had our first encounter, but the fact that we were in "public" didn't stop her from telling me about myself. (That's what she said: "I have some things to share, but first I need to tell you about yourself.") The rhetoric didn't make a ton of sense to me, but I rolled with it . . . which meant sitting there—in the corner booth we both prefer—and letting her blast me. Everything she said was true, but I'll do myself the favor of not writing down all the four-letter words she used.

When she was done, she excused herself to go to the bathroom and told me not to move. And I'm glad I listened. Because when she got back to the table, she thanked me. Said that even though I was an idiot, she also knew how sweet I can be. "I've been involved with some <u>truly</u> monstrous human beings," she said. "You made some grotesquely privileged and entitled decisions. But I believe your dickishness is partially a function of your trash conditioning, and I can tell you really do want to be less awful." (A backhanded compliment, if I've ever heard one.)

She also said that she could tell—could FEEL, even—that I really do care about her. And that despite my more-or-less "stealing" what she's sure would've been a victory for her, getting booted from the election was the best thing for her because she was "running for the wrong reasons and really hasn't healed enough from the other situation to actually be a good leader." (I knew all this from Avis, of course, but it was a slight weight off to hear Dylan confirm it.)

After telling me she hopes my loss "felt like a swift kick in the nuts from karma" (pulls no punches, this beautiful young woman), she let me know she wrote herself a love letter once she could comfortably flex her fingers again after attacking me. ("Which I'm not at all sorry about, even though I know violence isn't supposed to be the answer.")

That letter helped her see "that everything went the way it needed to" and she is "worthy of [her] OWN respect, honor, love, and dignity."

So I figured I'd give something similar a try.

Man, I sure am long-winded when talking to myself, huh?
Anyway, here goes.

Dear Jared,

Now I'm writing a letter to myself <u>within</u> a letter to myself, but I'm not going to get hung up on that. The truth is, I don't know you very well. I know who you've been told you should be by different entities—society and your dad included—but as evidenced by the amount of cognitive dissonance you've been experiencing since your best friend was shot and killed by a police officer two years ago, who you've been told to be doesn't seem to fit who you currently are or how you want to show up.

There are good things about you, for sure: You're generally smart, you do a decent job with critical thinking (most of the time), and you genuinely, if imperfectly, care about other people. You truly want to do good in the world. Make it better. How, you're not sure yet, but there is something to be said for your heart being in it for real.

There are also some not-so-great things. You make <u>powerfully</u> stupid decisions sometimes. This is because you don't take potential consequences seriously: More frequently than you'd care to admit, you've been able to evade them. You can also be pretty narrow-minded, you're often guilty of lots of talk with little action, you sometimes prefer to ignore certain truths about injustice and inequity because they don't affect you, and if we're being <u>completely</u> honest, there are times when the thought of giving up your advantages, even the ones you didn't earn, seems absolutely ludicrous to you. (I mean, seriously, who in their right mind would do that voluntarily?)

However, please receive this letter as my commitment to do better by you, get firm in what we value, and fully commit to it. Because we're stuck together literally for life. And I really do want to be at peace with you.

What does that look like? I'm not sure yet. But we're going to figure it out together, you and me.

And I think I know a good place to start:

We will not let the opinions of people who don't recognize the inherent value in ALL human beings impact our view of ourself or hold sway over how we move through the world.

In layman's terms: We're no longer going to let people we don't even like impact how we feel about ourself and our decisions. Dad included. (Because "keeping it a hundred," as Justyce would say, we love the man but we certainly don't LIKE him. Also, keeping up with these first-person plural pronouns is making our head hurt, so I'm going back to second.)

You're an okay guy, Jared. I really believe that. And working your way toward being good. You're not there yet, but you've come a long way, and I'm proud of you.

Let's keep it up, yeah?

Sincerely,
Jared

P.S. Dude, you totally dropped the ball on getting the girl. I'll forgive you this time, but let's do better. Like, come on, man.

ACT IV

Second-in-Command

Two weeks later

There are two things Jared Peter Christensen is sure of. The first is that Ainsley Cruz might not be so bad after all. No, he still doesn't want to date her. But he certainly respects her more after learning that despite being the person who sent him the Dylan mug shots, she didn't share them with anyone else. ("My goal was to give *you* an advantage, not ruin a fellow ambitious woman's reputation.")

The second thing he's sure of is his relief at being done with finals. His second year of undergrad is officially over, and though not everything went as he hoped it would, he can safely say he's a different man than the one who stepped on campus at the top of first semester.

He's fairly certain he crushed it and will be able to maintain his excellent grades in his four courses that involved an actual end-of-course exam, but he'd be lying if he said the one that had a final project instead—Constitutional Law with Dr. Yeh—didn't have him worried about losing his grip on that 3.97 GPA he's been able to maintain thus far.

As it turns out, though, he needn't have worried. By the time he gets back to the apartment he shares with his best friend, Justyce McAllister—who may be the best overall human on earth—there's an email notification: His and Dylan's grade on their Constitutional Law project final has been posted on the class website.

It doesn't occur to Jared that "posted on the class website" means *anyone* who took the class will be able to see said grade until he clicks the Final Project Assessment tab and realizes he can see *everyone's* grade.

A total menace to conventionality, that Dr. Yeh.

He smiles, though. His grade, which is near the top of the alphabetical-by-surname list: 92. And Dylan got a 95. (Guess Dr. Yeh really did take those partner evaluations seriously: He wrote Dylan a *glowing* review and admitted she did the bulk of the work, as a part of his commitment to being more honest with himself and others.)

His first thought is to call Dylan and thank her . . . but his curiosity gets the better of him. He keeps scrolling through the project scores.

"Whoa," he says when he reaches *LePlante IV, John Preston.* Jared can't remember who John Preston's partner was, but John Preston got the lowest grade out of both sections: 67.

Despite knowing it's classic schadenfreude, Jared smiles. No clue what his other final grades will be, and he knows it's not technically a competition. But *damn,* does it feel good to so thoroughly own his proverbial nemesis.

Jared drops onto the comfy couch in his and Justyce's shared living room and clasps his hands behind his head. He feels pretty good, all things considered. His phone double-buzzes with a notification . . . which catches him off guard. He assigned that particular alert to messages in the UCC portal and hasn't heard it since the election results came in.

He opens it. There's a direct message to him from Ari Park: *Need to meet ASAP.*

Weird.

He's typing out a response when his phone pings with a text. It's from Avis—

But before he can open *that,* the thing starts buzzing, and "Int'l Players Anthem" blasts into the air.

Amir.

Jared cautiously lifts the phone to his ear. "Hello?"

"DUDE!" Amir hollers. "¡Escándalo!"

"Bro, what are you—"

The phone *boops* with another incoming call. It's Pat Neuman.

"Hold just one sec, A.T.—"

"What do you mean, *hold*? Do you have any idea how monumental this is?!"

"I actually *don't* because you haven't said anything of substance. One sec."

"JARE—"

He switches to the other call. "Pat?"

"DUDE!" Pat says. "Twins and Aaron are with me right now! WE SHOULD'VE KNOWN, MAN!"

Now Jared is starting to get frustrated. What the hell is everyone going on about?!

"I know, right?" Jared says, feigning agreement. "Hey, let me call you back in a few. Amir's on the other line."

Pat: "'Course, man."

"You know we'll be here!" Robbie (or is it Roger?) yells from the background.

Jared returns to Amir's call. "You've got seven seconds to tell me what's going on, Amir—with zero guessing games and no embellishments. Otherwise, I hang up and never speak to you again."

"Sheesh, man, you don't gotta be so touchy—"

"You're down to four, A.T.!"

"Fine, fine!" Amir says. "Word on the quad is that your good pal John Preston LePlante IV has gotten himself into some Sugar Honey Iced Tea."

"Some *what?*" from Jared.

"It's an acronym. You'll figure it out. Anyway, he's been implicated as the leader in one hell of an AI cheating ring."

Wait . . . "Say *what* now?"

"And if my sources are correct, he's been stripped of the right to participate in *any* on-campus organizations—athletics and UCC included—and is on the brink of expulsion."

Jared is speechless.

"No clue what the UCC's policy is for something like this. They may not have one—as you know, I did my due diligence and read the election and governing parameters thoroughly, and I don't recall seeing anything that would address this directly. However, it would only make sense that if the president-elect (a) is unable to take office and (b) hasn't selected a VP, the mantle of said office would pass to the candidate who technically 'lost' the election—"

Jared's phone beeps in his ear again. It's Dylan this time. Certainly not missing this one . . .

"A.T., I gotta put you on hold again."

"BRO!" he replies. "Are you not *hearing* what I'm *saying*? I'm pretty sure *you* are the new JCC pres—"

"Just hold *on*!"

Jared doesn't know why he's resistant to what Amir is trying to tell him. Perhaps the implications are too much to digest.

As he takes a deep breath and switches over to the other line, the reality settles onto Jared's shoulders: There's a solid chance that despite *losing* the election, Jared Peter Christensen is the new Junior Class Council president.

Doing his best to stay calm, he lifts the phone to his ear. "Hello?"

Dylan Marie Coleman says only two words:

"You ready?"

Author's Note

Well, hey!

If you're reading this, I'm going to presume you got all the way through Jared's story and are just *desperate* for more. Sadly, more will not be forthcoming, but I do want to take this space and make a confession: This book was immaculately terrifying to write. Even more so than *Dear Martin.*

Why? Well, for one, I'm not a white boy.

Did I grow up drowning in them? Yes. (For instance: Pat Neuman is a real dude, and we've been friends since our days in the back row of Ms. Welch's fifth-grade class at Peachtree Elementary. He really did do a couple of summer semesters at Morehouse, and to this day, he's one of my favorite people on the planet.)

Was I confident I could write from a white boy's perspective (in mostly third-person present tense, which did give me a *little* distance to work with)? I was.

But that didn't mean *you*, dear reader, would buy in. Especially considering how weird the world was at the time of my writing: As of June 2024, the first two *Dear* books have been resoundingly banned across the country, and legislation around public education has made it increasingly difficult for students to engage with topics like some of the ones addressed in *this* book, especially when the main character is Black.

So, I wrote a white boy instead.

There's a quote attributed to Toni Morrison: "The ability of writers to imagine what is not the self, to familiarize the strange and mystify the familiar, is the test of their power." Are there questions of history and power and politics and money when it comes to who is permitted to *profit* from telling stories that are not their own? Of course there are.

But I won't get into all that here.

What I will say: I also think this *imagining of what is not the self* is the test of our capacity for *true* empathy as well as an opportunity to dig down to the core of a shared humanity. And that was the scariest part of all: knowing I was actively humanizing a character that readers of *Dear Martin* love to hate. The question that churned in my brain as I wrote: Would readers hate *me* for not hating Jared? For *caring* about him, even? For *loving* him and holding space for him to be a person too?

I clearly pushed past all that and wrote the thing. I had to. Even just based on something Justyce says toward the end: The only person I gotta spend the rest of my life with is me. So, I couldn't *not* write it.

All that said, I deeply appreciate you taking the time to read it. Hopefully, it challenged you the way writing it challenged me.

—Nic

P.S. That thing about the Black teacher getting fired by his Black principal for teaching a Black-authored book about a Black character to a class of mostly Black kids during Black History Month because a white parent complained about it? True story. The book in question was *Dear Martin*.

P.P.S. Jared does make Dylan his VP.

P.P.P.S. I don't know if they wind up together. Neither of them has told me. ☺

Acknowledgments

There are a million and one people I could thank for the existence of this book, and in lieu of not forgetting—and therefore offending—anyone, I'm going to keep these acknowledgments super low-key:

Phoebe: We did it again! Thank you for believing in me on this one and sticking through the struggle bus part of its creation. You remain a wizard of an editor, and I'm so grateful to be working with you. Mollie: Your belief in me and willingness to go to bat for me are second to none. Thank you for just being who you are and going hard in the paint on my behalf. Avis, Pat, and Karo: Thank you for allowing me to immortalize you in fiction. You all make excellent book characters, if I do say so myself. Korey, Natalya, Wyatt, Dustin, and Jabari: Thank you for reading this thing early. And Mrs. Penny Kittle: Thank *you* for not only reading it early, but also suggesting I add a prologue.

Nigel: You continue to support my dreams by managing our small spawn, and I super appreciate you for that. Brittany: You never ever stop rooting for me and telling me I CAN DO IT and expressing your excitement about my work. I know I roll my eyes, but know that I'm listening, and I do believe you. And Angel: Thank you not only for your unwavering moral support and encouragement, but also for the provision of a quiet workspace and food and hydration when I'm in the zone. You're such a gift to me and the Most Excellent Judy.

About the Author

NIC STONE is the author of many novels, including the #1 *New York Times* bestseller *Dear Martin* and its *New York Times* bestselling sequel *Dear Justyce*. She also penned the young adult titles *Odd One Out,* an NPR Best Book and an ALA Rainbow Book Top Ten; *Jackpot,* a YALSA Quick Pick Selection, and *Chaos Theory,* a YALSA Best Fiction Book for Young Adults Reading List selection. Her middle-grade novels include *Clean Getaway,* a *New York Times* bestseller, and *Fast Pitch,* a YALSA Quick Pick Selection. Nic lives in Atlanta and will continue to ruffle feathers with her writing.

nicstone.info

Catch up on Nic Stone's spellbinding
debut—a #1 *New York Times* bestseller!

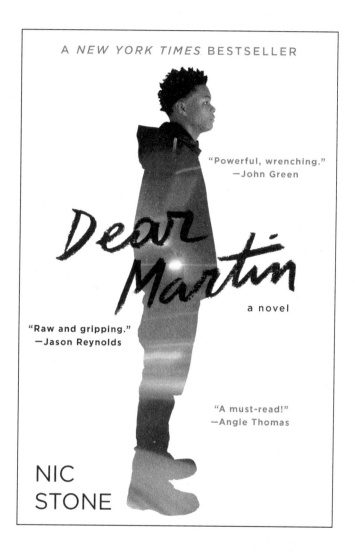

A *NEW YORK TIMES* BESTSELLER

"Powerful, wrenching."
—John Green

Dear Martin

a novel

"Raw and gripping."
—Jason Reynolds

"A must-read!"
—Angie Thomas

NIC
STONE

CHAPTER 1

From where he's standing across the street, Justyce can see her: Melo Taylor, ex-girlfriend, slumped over beside her Benz on the damp concrete of the FarmFresh parking lot. She's missing a shoe, and the contents of her purse are scattered around her like the guts of a pulled party popper. He knows she's stone drunk, but this is too much, even for her.

Jus shakes his head, remembering the judgment all over his best friend Manny's face as he left Manny's house not fifteen minutes ago.

The WALK symbol appears.

As he approaches, she opens her eyes, and he waves and pulls his earbuds out just in time to hear her say, "What the hell are you doing here?"

Justyce asks himself the same question as he watches her try—and fail—to shift to her knees. She falls over sideways and hits her face against the car door.

He drops down and reaches for her cheek—which is as

red as the candy-apple paint job. "Damn, Melo, are you okay?"

She pushes his hand away. "What do you care?"

Stung, Justyce takes a deep breath. He cares a lot. Obviously. If he didn't, he wouldn't've walked a mile from Manny's house at three in the morning (Manny's of the opinion that Melo's "the worst thing that ever happened" to Jus, so of course he refused to give his boy a ride). All to keep his drunken disaster of an ex from driving.

He should walk away right now, Justyce should.

But he doesn't.

"Jessa called me," he tells her.

"That skank—"

"Don't be like that, babe. She only called me because she cares about you."

Jessa had planned to take Melo home herself, but Mel threatened to call the cops and say she'd been kidnapped if Jessa didn't drop her at her car.

Melo can be a little dramatic when she's drunk.

"I'm totally unfollowing her," she says (case in point). "In life *and* online. Nosy bitch."

Justyce shakes his head again. "I just came to make sure you get home okay." That's when it hits Justyce that while he might succeed in getting Melo home, he has no idea how he'll get back. He closes his eyes as Manny's words ring through his head: *This Captain Save-A-Ho thing is gonna get you in trouble, dawg.*

He looks Melo over. She's now sitting with her head leaned back against the car door, half-asleep, mouth open.

He sighs. Even drunk, Jus can't deny Melo's the finest girl he's ever laid eyes on not to mention *hands*—on.

She starts to tilt, and Justyce catches her by the shoulders to keep her from falling. She startles, looking at him wide-eyed, and Jus can see everything about her that initially caught his attention. Melo's dad is this Hall of Fame NFL linebacker (biiiiig black dude), but her mom is from Norway. She got Mrs. Taylor's milky Norwegian complexion, wavy hair the color of honey, and amazing green eyes that are kind of purple around the edge, but she has really full lips, a small waist, crazy curvy hips, and probably the nicest butt Jus has ever seen in his life.

That's part of his problem: he gets too tripped up by how beautiful she is. He never would've dreamed a girl as fine as her would be into *him*.

Now he's got the urge to kiss her even though her eyes are red and her hair's a mess and she smells like vodka and cigarettes and weed. But when he goes to push her hair out of her face, she shoves his hand away again. "Don't touch me, Justyce."

She starts shifting her stuff around on the ground—lipstick, Kleenex, tampons, one of those circular thingies with the makeup in one half and a mirror in the other, a flask. "Ugh, where are my keeeeeeeys?"

Justyce spots them in front of the back tire and snatches them up. "You're not driving, Melo."

"Give 'em." She swipes for the keys but falls into his arms instead. Justyce props her against the car again and gathers the rest of her stuff to put it back in her bag—

which is large enough to hold a week's worth of groceries (what is it with girls and purses the size of duffel bags?). He unlocks the car, tosses the bag on the floor of the backseat, and tries to get Melo up off the ground.

Then everything goes really wrong, really fast.

First, she throws up all over the hoodie Jus is wearing.

Which belongs to Manny. Who specifically said, "Don't come back here with throw-up on my hoodie."

Perfect.

Jus takes off the sweatshirt and tosses it in the backseat.

When he tries to pick Melo up again, she slaps him. Hard. "Leave me *alone*, Justyce," she says.

"I can't do that, Mel. There's no way you'll make it home if you try to drive yourself."

He tries to lift her by the armpits and she spits in his face.

He considers walking away again. He could call her parents, stick her keys in his pocket, and bounce. Oak Ridge is probably *the* safest neighborhood in Atlanta. She'd be fine for the twenty-five minutes it would take Mr. Taylor to get here.

But he can't. Despite Manny's assertion that Melo needs to "suffer some consequences for once," leaving her here all vulnerable doesn't seem like the right thing to do. So he picks her up and tosses her over his shoulder.

Melo responds in her usual delicate fashion: she screams and beats him on the back with her fists.

Don't miss the sensational follow-up to
#1 *New York Times* bestseller and
William C. Morris Award finalist *Dear Martin*!

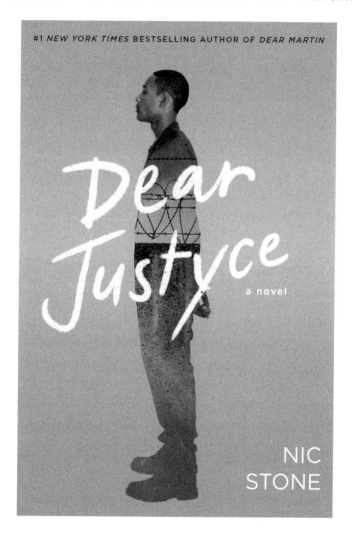

Snapshot:

Two Boys on
a Brand-New
Playground
(2010)

It didn't take much for Quan to decide he was leaving this time. He feels a little bit bad, yeah: knowing Dasia and Gabe are still in the house makes his stomach hurt the way it always does when he finds himself faced with grown-people problems he can't fix. But Quan's only nine. Running away *alone* is hard enough. Trying to bring a four-year-old sister and a two-year-old brother just isn't gonna work.

He's glad spring has sprung early. Didn't have time to grab a jacket as he fled. He's pretty sure there was too much commotion for anybody to notice, but he takes a few unnecessary turns en route to his destination in case Olaf—that's what Quan calls his mama's "duck-ass boyfriend" (which is what Quan's *dad* calls the guy)—*did* notice Quan's exit.

What Quan is sure of? He couldn't stay there. Not with dude yelling and throwing things the way he was. Quan knows what comes next, and he couldn't watch again. It was hard enough seeing the aftermath bloom in the funny-looking bluey-purple blotches that made Mama's arms and legs look like someone had tossed water balloons full of paint all over her. He couldn't really do anything anyway. Though Olaf (Dwight is the guy's *actual* name) isn't *too*, too big, he's a whole heck of a lot stronger than Quan. The one time Quan did try to intervene, he wound up with his own funky-colored blotch. Across his lower back from where he hit the dining room table when dude literally threw Quan across the room.

Hiding that bruise from Daddy was nearly impossible. And Quan *had* to hide it because he knew if Daddy found out what really happened when Olaf/Dwight came around . . . well, it wouldn't be good.

So. He made sure Dasia and Gabe were safe in the closet. That was the most he could do.

As Wynwood Heights Park looms up on his left, Quan lifts the hem of his shirt to wipe his face. It's the fourth time he's done it, so there's a wet spot now. He wonders if there will be any dry spots left by the time he gets the tears to stop. Good thing there's no one around to see. He'd never hear the end of it.

He bounces on his toes as his feet touch down on the springy stuff the new playground is built on. There's a sign that says it's ground-up old tires, that the play structures are made from "recycled water bottles and other discarded plastics," and that the entire area is "green," but as Dasia pointed out the last time Mama brought them all here, whoever built the thing didn't know their colors because everything is red, yellow, and blue.

The thought of his sass-mouthed little sister brings fresh tears to Quan's eyes.

He makes a beeline for the rocket ship. It sits off in a

corner separate from everything else, tip pointed at the sky like it could blast off at any moment. Inside the cylindrical base, there are buttons to push and dials to turn and a ladder that leads up to an "observation deck" with a little window. It's Quan's favorite spot in the world—though he'd never admit that to anyone.

When he gets inside, he's so relieved, he collapses against the rounded wall and lets his body slide to the floor like chocolate ice cream down the side of a cone on a hot summer day. His head drops back, and he shuts his eyes and lets the tears flow freely.

But then there's a sound above him. A cough.

The moonlight through the deck window makes the face of the boy staring down at Quan look kinda ghostly. In fact, the longer dude stares without speaking, the more Quan wonders if maybe he *is* a ghost.

"Uhhh . . . hello?"

Dude doesn't reply.

Now Quan is starting to get creeped out. Which makes him mad. This is supposed to be the one place in the world he can *relax*. Where he's not looking over his shoulder or being extra cautious. Where he can close his eyes and count down from ten and imagine shooting into space, far, far away from everything and everyone.

"Yo, why you lookin' at me like that?" Quan spits, each word sharp-tipped and laced with the venom of his rage.

"Oh, umm . . ." The other boy's eyes drop to his hands.